Acting Edition

The Moors

by Jen Silverman

SAMUEL FRENCH

ISBN 978-0-573-70540-3

www.concordtheatricals.com
www.concordtheatricals.co.uk

FOR PRODUCTION INQUIRIES

UNITED STATES AND CANADA
info@concordtheatricals.com
1-866-979-0447

UNITED KINGDOM AND EUROPE
licensing@concordtheatricals.co.uk
020-7054-7298

Each title is subject to availability from Concord Theatricals Corp., depending upon country of performance. Please be aware that *THE MOORS* may not be licensed by Concord Theatricals Corp. in your territory. Professional and amateur producers should contact the nearest Concord Theatricals Corp. office or licensing partner to verify availability.

This work is published by Samuel French, an imprint of
Concord Theatricals Corp.

THE MOORS premiered at Yale Repertory Theatre in February 2016. It was directed by Jackson Gay, with set design by Alexander Woodward, costume design by Fabian Fidel Aguilar, lighting design by Andrew F. Griffin, sound design and song composition by Daniel Kluger, and fight choreography by Rick Sordelet. The cast was as follows:

AGATHA .... Kelly McAndrew
HULDEY .... Birgit Huppuch
EMILIE .... Miriam Silverman
MARJORY .... Hannah Cabell
THE MASTIFF .... Jeff Biehl
A MOOR-HEN .... Jessica Love

THE MOORS received its New York premiere with The Playwrights Realm in February 2017. It was directed by Mike Donahue, with set design by Dane Laffrey, costume design by Anita Yavich, lighting design by Jen Schriever, sound design by M.L. Dogg, song composition by Daniel Kluger, and fight choreography by J. Allen Suddeth. The cast was as follows:

AGATHA .... Linda Powell
HULDEY .... Birgit Huppuch
EMILIE .... Chasten Harmon
MARJORY .... Hannah Cabell
THE MASTIFF .... Andrew Garman
A MOOR-HEN .... Teresa Avia Lim

CHARACTERS

AGATHA – Female. Elder spinster sister. Spidery. Dangerous. Powerful.

HULDEY – Female. Younger spinster sister. She has a diary. She wants to be famous.

EMILIE – Female. The governess. A romantic with a sweet face.

MARJORY – Female. The scullery maid. Down-trodden. Strategic.

THE MASTIFF – Male. The dog. A sad philosopher-king.

A MOOR-HEN – Female. A small chicken. Practical and very present-tense.

SETTING

The bleak moors...of England?

Think *Wuthering Heights* and *Jane Eyre* and the Brontë sisters.

However: the characters all have American accents (or accents native to the country of production). Play the anachronisms. This play is about the present.

TIME

The 1840s...ish

PLAYWRIGHT'S NOTES

Casting is best when very diverse. The sisters do not have to be played by actors of the same ethnicity. There is *no* version in which *only* the animals are played by actors of color.

[ ] is unspoken, although the character is thinking it.
( ) is spoken out loud but is a side-thought.

MUSIC NOTE

"Huldey's Power Ballad": The lead sheet included at the back of this Acting Edition is for rehearsal only. For performance, licensees are provided with a performance package that includes tracks and a full orchestration. The song can be performed with either tracked or live musical accompaniment.

"Emilie's Song": The Lute/Vocal Score included at the back of the Acting Edition is intended for both rehearsal and performance. This music is also included in a performance package provided to licensees. The song is intended to be performed with live musical accompaniment.

1.

(Thud!)

(The sound of a horrible impact that shakes our world – a bird-body hitting glass.)

(Lights up on the parlor of an elegant, ancient mansion on the English moors. 1840-ish, to a degree.)

*(***AGATHA** *looms over* **HULDEY**. *She pulls at* **HULDEY***'s clothes, adjusts her hair.* **HULDEY** *stands like a doll and lets herself be manipulated.)*

(The maid, **MARJORY**, *stands to the side, waiting to be useful.* **MARJORY** *is wearing a parlor maid hat, but when she is the scullery maid, she will put on a different hat. There is only one maid in this household.)*

(The dog, a giant **MASTIFF**, *stares despondently out the window and thinks about how meaningless everything always seems to be.)*

AGATHA. Something has to be done.

MARJORY. Yes ma'am.

AGATHA. Every time one sits in the parlor, one must endure a bird crashing into the window.

MARJORY. It's terrible, ma'am.

AGATHA. See that you do something about it.

MARJORY. What would you like me to do?

AGATHA. Fix it, of course. Why am I the only one around here who takes it upon myself to fix things?

(Tugging **HULDEY***'s hair.)*

AGATHA. Do you think this is acceptable?

HULDEY. ...No?

AGATHA. No, sister, it is not.

Do you know why your hair is not acceptable?

HULDEY. ...No?

AGATHA. It looks like the location a particularly mangy bird might choose to nest. Do you think this is the sort of hair one wishes to have on the day the governess arrives?

HULDEY. *(She knows the answer to this one!)* No!

AGATHA. No, it is not that sort of hair.

What on earth have you been doing all morning?

HULDEY. *(A flash of hope, she definitely knows the answer.)* Oh! Well –

AGATHA. Don't answer that.

*(**HULDEY** subsides. To **MARJORY**:)*

Is the extra room made up for the governess?

MARJORY. Yes ma'am.

AGATHA. And is there Moor-Hen for tonight?

MARJORY. *(Isn't sure.)* Well...uh...

AGATHA. Why don't you ask the scullery maid.

MARJORY. Yes ma'am.

*(She is gone. The **MASTIFF** raises his head.)*

*(He looks at **AGATHA**.)*

AGATHA. *(Steely.)* Down.

*(The **MASTIFF** lowers his head again.)*

HULDEY. Agatha...?

AGATHA. What is it.

HULDEY. Why is there a governess coming?

(A strict beat.)

AGATHA. Huldeygard.

HULDEY. Yes?

AGATHA. How is it possible that you haven't washed your face?

(She spit-polishes **HULDEY***'s face.)*

HULDEY. Well, this morning –

AGATHA. Don't answer that.

*(***MARJORY** *returns.)*

MARJORY. The cook is making Moor-Hen, and also there are potatoes, and also the scullery maid has the typhus again.

AGATHA. Ask her if she has any sisters.

MARJORY. Sisters?

AGATHA. If she dies, perhaps one of her sisters might replace her.

MARJORY. Yes ma'am.

*(***MARJORY** *leaves.)*

HULDEY. *(Faintly, but with daring.)* You see, this morning I didn't have time to wash my face.

AGATHA. You might as well be a wild animal.

HULDEY. I was writing in my diary, you see.

AGATHA. You might as well live out on the moors with the tiny smudgy weasels.

HULDEY. And I'd reached a good part.

AGATHA. A "good part."

HULDEY. *(Fainter.)* ...Of my...uh...diary?

AGATHA. If one is not writing sums and lists and possibly strategies, then I do not know what one is writing.

HULDEY. *(Brightly, taking this as an invitation.)* Oh, well, I was just writing about –

AGATHA. Don't answer that.

(A beat.)

I've been nourishing the hope that, since father's death, you might turn your attention to more pressing matters. You are used to having everything done for you. Father spoiled you, Branwell spoiled you, but I have no intention of spoiling you, sister.

*(**MARJORY** returns.)*

MARJORY. Pardon me, Miss.

AGATHA. Yes, Mallory?

MARJORY. The scullery maid has five sisters, two of whom are quite homely, two of whom are feverish, one of whom is bilious, and also there is a carriage in the driveway, it has just arrived.

AGATHA. Ah.

HULDEY. *(Overwhelmed with excitement.)* The governess!

AGATHA. Show her in.

MARJORY. Yes ma'am.

*(**MARJORY** leaves. **HULDEY**, somewhat downtrodden, is lifted by a new wave of excitement.)*

HULDEY. Do you think she might be very pretty? And do you think she might like to read, perhaps she might keep a diary –?

AGATHA. If she does, we shall break her of that immediately.

*(The **MASTIFF** raises his head, also excited.)*

Down.

*(Both **HULDEY** and the **MASTIFF** sit down, eyes trained on the door. A beat of steely silence.)*

*(**MARJORY** enters with **EMILIE** in tow. **EMILIE** wears a travelling cloak. She is on her best behavior and very much wants to be liked. She carries a case for a lute [or other string instrument].)*

MARJORY. Miss Agatha, Miss Huldey, may I present the governess.

EMILIE. *(A little breathless.)* Why hello. I'm *so* pleased to make your acquaintance, you must be...? Mistress Agatha. Mistress... Huldey. Master Branwell...?

(Looks around, doesn't see him.)

Oh! Well. A dog! Very large dog! Nice doggy.

(The **MASTIFF** *raises his head and looks at her hopefully.)*

I love dogs.

AGATHA. *(Cold.)* It is dangerous.

EMILIE. Ah yes?

AGATHA. It is very large and very dangerous. You must never touch it.

(The **MASTIFF** *looks at* **AGATHA** *dolefully. She hisses. He puts his head back down.)*

EMILIE. Oh.

AGATHA. You, I presume, are Miss Vandergaard.

EMILIE. Oh! Manners! Pardon. Yes. Emilie Vandergaard, governess. In your service, I'm *so* pleased. What a long journey it's been, you must forgive me, I'm slightly scattered.

(She laughs, airy and delightful.)

*(***AGATHA** *sizes her up.)*

HULDEY. *(Re: the instrument case.)* ...What's that?

EMILIE. This? Why, it's a lute.

HULDEY. Do you play music?

EMILIE. For the children, yes, I play lullabies sometimes.

HULDEY. *(Overawed.)* Nobody ever sang to me.

AGATHA. *(Breaking in, cool.)* How was your trip, Miss Vandergaard?

EMILIE. Oh, it was fine, no problems at all, a little long maybe but –

AGATHA. I'm delighted. We've been waiting for you.

EMILIE. I'm absolutely enchanted to be here.

HULDEY. Did you come from London?

EMILIE. Well, I passed through it.

HULDEY. How was it?

EMILIE. It was very big.

HULDEY. *(Soft, to* **EMILIE.***)* I'd like to see London.

AGATHA. Miss Vandergaard has only just arrived, and I'm sure she has no time to discuss...*London.*

(To **EMILIE.***)*

Sit.

*(***HULDEY** *subsides.* **EMILIE** *sits.)*

*(***EMILIE** *gives the* **MASTIFF** *a tentative smile. He stares at her, mournful, without moving.)*

It will devour your face.

EMILIE. Oh!

That's dreadful!

Has it always been so savage?

AGATHA. *(Decisively.)* Yes, always.

Things around here are savage things.

The moors are a savage place, and we who live here, despite our attempts to cling to a modicum of civilization, we find ourselves often forced to contend with savagery. Are you sure you're up for the task, Miss Vandergaard?

EMILIE. Oh, call me Emilie.

AGATHA. *Miss* Vandergaard?

EMILIE. I – well – I've been a governess many times before, if that's what you mean – I did send Master Branwell several references in my letter?

(She glances around again.)

Master Branwell must be out at the moment, I imagine?

AGATHA. He must be.

EMILIE. And children have always – well, I do like to think they have felt tender affections toward me – but most importantly, Miss Agatha, discipline has never been an issue.

*(***AGATHA** *just stares at her. Sizing her up.)*

Perhaps if Master Branwell is out on a walk I might – or if he's with the horses I might just – an introduction, or a friendly hello, or –

AGATHA. I'm afraid that's not possible.

EMILIE. Not...? Oh. Of course.

(Pause.)

Master Branwell was kind in his letters, he spoke very highly of his sisters.

AGATHA. *(Decisively.)* Miss Vandergaard.

EMILIE. Yes?

AGATHA. Dinner is always served promptly at six. One hopes not to be late for dinner.

EMILIE. Will Master Branwell be at dinner?

*(**HULDEY** looks at **AGATHA**. **AGATHA** does not even respond to the glance.)*

AGATHA. Master Branwell has been unwell.

EMILIE. Oh I'm so sorry. That's terrible.

AGATHA. Master Branwell may not be at dinner.

EMILIE. And the child?

*(**HULDEY** looks at **AGATHA** again.)*

AGATHA. The child. Eats in the nursery. With a maid.

EMILIE. I'm so looking forward to meeting him.

AGATHA. It is also dangerous.

EMILIE. Pardon me?

AGATHA. It is undisciplined, I said. Children of the moors are undisciplined children.

The maid will show you to your room.

*(**MARJORY** coughs. It's a wet, horrible cough.)*

*(She stares at **EMILIE** as she coughs.)*

EMILIE. Oh!

HULDEY. *(Brightly, confiding.)* Marjory is the scullery maid. She has the typhus, you know.

EMILIE. Oh no!

HULDEY. And the parlor maid is Mallory. She's with child.

EMILIE. Oh my!

AGATHA. That will be all. Thank you.

EMILIE. *(Stands, curtseys.)* I'm so pleased. Really quite. Grateful to be in the employ of such. Old and well-bred. Ancestral home.

AGATHA. Yes yes. Until dinner.

MARJORY. This way.

*(**MARJORY** leads **EMILIE** out. A moment.)*

HULDEY. *(Wistful.)* This will all be such fun.

AGATHA. It will be many things, sister.

*(**AGATHA** leaves the room. **HULDEY** follows.)*

*(A moment. Then the **MASTIFF** raises his head. He stares out the window at the moors.)*

MASTIFF. A bird drops from the sky
like a stone in the stomach
like all your happiness
fleeting, then gone.
The gorse extends
the sky extends
many things extend.
Happiness, I suppose, does not extend.
I was once upon a time, greatly satisfied.
I believe. I do not remember clearly.
I put my face against my mother's side.
There was milk.
I imagine this caused me satisfaction.
I would not presume to call it..."happiness."

(Beat – sadly.)

There is nothing lasting in this world.
Birds drop and drop
there are always more
the sky keeps spitting out birds

and the birds keep dropping.
In that sense, you might say: birds are lasting, in this world.
To which I would reply: it is never the same bird.

2.

*(**EMILIE**'s bedroom, that seems to be the exact same room as the parlor. **MARJORY** leads **EMILIE** in, coughing from time to time. It's a deeply jarring machine-gun noise.)*

MARJORY. And this will be your bedroom.

EMILIE. Oh...uh...

MARJORY. Is there a problem?

EMILIE. ...Is this not the parlor?

MARJORY. It's your bedroom. Ma'am.

EMILIE. ...Oh, but, you see, it looks like...?

*(She trails away under **MARJORY**'s baleful eye.)*

I see. Yes. Of course.

(A beat.)

MARJORY. Mistress Agatha asked to see you were settled. You look settled.

(She puts on her scullery maid cap.)

Now there's dishes to attend to in the scullery.

EMILIE. Just a moment.

MARJORY. Yes ma'am?

EMILIE. Which maid did you say you were?

MARJORY. *(Takes off the cap.)* I'm the maid. Your maid.

EMILIE. And you have the typhus?

MARJORY. Sort of everybody's maid.

Yes, yes I do.

EMILIE. Are you the one with the typhus, or the one with the baby?

MARJORY. I'm both, sort of both.

EMILIE. How are you both of something? Either you are something, or you are another thing.

MARJORY. When I'm in the scullery, I have the typhus.

When I'm in the parlor, I have the baby.

EMILIE. Oh.

MARJORY. It's how the time passes here.

EMILIE. I see. That is one way of doing things.

MARJORY. Indeed it is.

EMILIE. I'm terribly sorry to hear about your...conditions.

MARJORY. I don't need you to be.

(She turns to go again.)

EMILIE. Ah – just a moment?

MARJORY. Yes ma'am.

EMILIE. How long have you worked for this household?

MARJORY. Oh. Forever, ma'am.

EMILIE. How old are you?

MARJORY. I haven't been counting. Ma'am.

EMILIE. But you were raised out here on these savage moors, you were treated kindly, perhaps they took you to church on Sundays to hear their father's sermons...? Master Branwell said –

MARJORY. *(Alarmed.)* You spoke to him!

EMILIE. In the letter. He wrote me a letter.

MARJORY. *(Relieved, subsiding.)* Oh.

EMILIE. ...What surprises you?

MARJORY. Nothing. I'm not surprised.

EMILIE. You seem so. You seem greatly surprised.

MARJORY. No, not I.

(Stand-off.)

EMILIE. Is Master Branwell very frightening? Are you frightened of him?

*(**MARJORY** puts the scullery maid cap back on.)*

MARJORY. You'd have to ask the parlor maid about that.

(She leaves.)

(A moment. **EMILIE** *looks around the parlor/bedroom. She takes a letter out of her bosom pocket. She looks at it – inquiring, troubled.)*

(Footsteps, and **HULDEY** *slips in.)*

HULDEY. *(Girlish, mischievous.)* There you are!

EMILIE. *(Tucks the letter away.)* Mistress Huldey!

HULDEY. Forgive me for barging into your bedroom, I know you might want some time to refresh, but I couldn't help myself. I'm so excited you're here!

EMILIE. Oh – well – thank you...

HULDEY. I just know you'll love it here! The bracing air, and the strange thorny flowers, and the gorse... And there are lots of long walks you might take. Although there's quicksand of course, and also large ravenous birds, and if you walked too far you might get turned around and lost and starve to death, or you might even be eaten by something. But in general, the moors are very pretty.

(A beat.)

EMILIE. Mistress Huldey –

HULDEY. Oh, just Huldey, please.

EMILIE. Huldey –

HULDEY. It sounds so wonderful how you say my name.

EMILIE. Can I ask you something?

HULDEY. Anything!

EMILIE. ...Is this my bedroom?

HULDEY. *(Looks around, bewildered.)* Of course.

EMILIE. Ah.

But.

Does it not – I mean – does it not look *very much* like the parlor?

HULDEY. *(Blank.)* Does it?

(A beat – charging onward.)

– And father's parsonage is down the hill, and you shall like that. Agatha and I do still enjoy going there for the sermons, even though father's replacement is rather less exciting than father was. But! It will be such fun to go together, to sit side by side, we might share a hymnal, we might share gloves, we might share shoes! I have a diary.

EMILIE. ...I'm sorry?

HULDEY. *(Staring at her very intently now.)* A diary. I keep one.

EMILIE. Well that's lovely.

HULDEY. It is very exceedingly personal and private of course, I shouldn't like to tell you what I write in it. I have a very active imagination.

EMILIE. Master Branwell – is he also a man of God?

HULDEY. No, I wouldn't say that.

EMILIE. A kind man, would you say? A gentle one?

HULDEY. Do you keep a diary, Emilie? (May I call you Emilie?)

EMILIE. I don't keep a diary, I'm afraid.

HULDEY. Oh that's too bad. That's too bad. But you might start!

EMILIE. I...might, I suppose.

HULDEY. *(Delighted.)* You might start tonight, if you wanted.

EMILIE. I'm not much of a writer, I have to confess –

HULDEY. It's not hard at all, I could help you. What you do is, you begin with a heading: MONDAY, for example, and then you just write down what you feel. And when you have a different feeling, you write down a different header, TUESDAY, for example –

EMILIE. *(Laughing.)* But you can't just start a new day whenever you like.

HULDEY. Of course you can. That's how the time works out here.

EMILIE. ...Well, that's very helpful, I'll consider it.

If you don't mind my asking about your brother –

HULDEY. You might write about London, too. You might describe what it was like.

EMILIE. I – yes, I suppose I could.

HULDEY. And then you might read it to me. For example, I've heard that in London, one gets murdered.

EMILIE. Murdered?

HULDEY. Most horribly murdered, I've heard.

(A beat. **EMILIE** *tries again.)*

EMILIE. Would you describe your brother as a *gentle* man, do you think, Huldey?

HULDEY. My brother?

EMILIE. Yes.

HULDEY. Describe him?

EMILIE. For example – he had a very nice hand. In his letters.

HULDEY. Did he.

EMILIE. A very *gentle* and well-formed hand.

HULDEY. That's nice.

EMILIE. And the words he used were educated ones.

HULDEY. Yes, well.

There's lots of time out here. In which to be educated in one thing or another.

EMILIE. But I imagine your brother went to study somewhere? London, perhaps? France?

HULDEY. Ah. Well. Studying.

Master Branwell. Was not. Studying, was not.

Quite.

EMILIE. Just like a boy. I imagine he preferred lively debates about the law, and dances, perhaps?

HULDEY. Hmm.

EMILIE. I'm so looking forward to meeting your brother – and the child –

HULDEY. *(A little desperate.)* It will be so lovely to have another person here, one that one might talk to, might sit by the fire on a lonely night and just – I might read you a page or two from my diary, if you very much wished it.

EMILIE. *(Alarmed.)* That wouldn't be necessary, I'm sure.

HULDEY. It's very vivid and upsetting, and I might, I might, if you *very* much –

EMILIE. Oh, no –

HULDEY. Just one page, or two, or perhaps a chapter, or –

EMILIE. We should both get ready for dinner, don't you think?

HULDEY. *(Deeply disappointed.)* Oh.
Well.
Indeed.
I should.
Before dinner.

(She leaves.)

*(***EMILIE***, alone, even more bewildered.)*

3.

(The **MASTIFF**. *Out on the moors.)*

(He stares up at the sky.)

(The sky is bleak.)

(The light is very sharp and clear.)

(All of it extends forever.)

(Birds fly, high up and far away.)

(The **MASTIFF** *is utterly alone.)*

MASTIFF. The pursuit of the ephemeral.
There is joy in it. To be sure.
Your fingers close around the thing,
it eludes you,
you desire more,
more eludes you,
frustration and ecstasy are nearly the same sensation.
Whole religions are based on this.
Also, it appears, relationships.

(The **MASTIFF** *closes his eyes.)*

"God."
"Hello God."
This is called prayer.
I talk, and you are silent.
Whole relationships are based on this as well.

(A bird drops from the sky.)

(It is a **MOOR-HEN.**)

(It crash-lands.)

MOOR-HEN. Ahhhh!

MASTIFF. You!

MOOR-HEN. I hate this!

MASTIFF. God!

MOOR-HEN. Flying! It's the worst!

...Sorry?

MASTIFF. It's you!

MOOR-HEN. Do we know each other?

MASTIFF. *(Double-takes.)* You look like a moor-hen.

MOOR-HEN. I am a moor-hen.

MASTIFF. Are you God, and *also* a moor-hen?

MOOR-HEN. This is a very circuitous line of questioning.

MASTIFF. I'm confused.

MOOR-HEN. I am a moor-hen. I hate flying. It makes me queasy. I hate landing. Well. No. I hate the take-off and I also hate the landing, but the actual part where I'm in the air, albeit brief, is not as hateful to me. In general. What were you asking me?

MASTIFF. Are you God or are you a moor-hen?

MOOR-HEN. What is..."God."

MASTIFF. Or did God send you?

MOOR-HEN. Nobody sends me. I make my own decisions.

(Beat. They take each other in. Cautiously.)

This..."God." It lives in the sky?

MASTIFF. Did you see Him on your way down?

MOOR-HEN. Is it a very large bird?

MASTIFF. I don't think so.

MOOR-HEN. But you saw it fly over?

MASTIFF. No, He lives there. The father of my house knew Him intimately.

MOOR-HEN. *(Baffled.)* Were you going to eat "God"?

MASTIFF. No! No. I just wanted to talk.

MOOR-HEN. I don't understand you at all.

(She turns to go.)

MASTIFF. Wait!

MOOR-HEN. What is it?

MASTIFF. What do you think of happiness?

MOOR-HEN. Of what-now?

MASTIFF. Happiness?

MOOR-HEN. I don't know what that is.

MASTIFF. It's this feeling like a clench, like a fist, like right where your heart is but further underneath. It hurts and then it's gone, and then you want it again.

MOOR-HEN. So...indigestion.

MASTIFF. I don't think...

MOOR-HEN. Or hunger.

MASTIFF. Not exactly...

MOOR-HEN. Like in the winters when there aren't enough berries or seeds or anything really and the clench-knot-fist in your stomach area hurts. And then spring comes! And there are berries and seeds. And bugs. Fat grubby grubs. And it goes away.

MASTIFF. No.

MOOR-HEN. Oh.

Then...no.

(Turns to go.)

MASTIFF. Wait!

MOOR-HEN. Wait what!

MASTIFF. I just want to talk to you.

MOOR-HEN. You're very large. You look very large. You look like perhaps something that might eat me.

MASTIFF. I don't intend to.

MOOR-HEN. But you admit that you are very large?

MASTIFF. I guess so.

MOOR-HEN. Well, there you go.

(The **MOOR-HEN** *turns to go.)*

MASTIFF. I'm very lonely.

MOOR-HEN. You're...what-now?

MASTIFF. Lonely. It's that thing – that clench – that fist in your stomach except this time it *doesn't* go away, and you *don't* want it.

MOOR-HEN. You're hungry. And I'm small. And I think I should go now.

(The **MOOR-HEN** *leaves.)*

(The **MASTIFF** *sits alone.)*

MASTIFF. Well.
That didn't go very well.
The moors swallow all the sound.
We don't even hear our own intentions, after a time.
We're just filled with the sound
of things getting lost.

4.

(After dinner, in the Second Sitting Room... which appears to be the same room as the parlor. **AGATHA** *crochets.* **HULDEY** *and* **EMILIE** *sip tea.* **MARJORY** *serves the tea. She wears a parlor maid hat. The* **MASTIFF** *lies by the window.)*

HULDEY. Dinner is very spare. Most things here, you'll find, are spare.

EMILIE. Oh no, not at all.

HULDEY. I'm sure it's not what you're used to.

EMILIE. I don't mind in the slightest.

HULDEY. But it is rather nice to sit in the Second Sitting Room after dinner, we so rarely use it. Isn't it nice?

EMILIE. *(Sotto.)* ...Are we not in the parlor?

HULDEY. *(Confused.)* No, this is the Second Sitting Room.

EMILIE. ...Oh.

HULDEY. You've been all over, haven't you. How wonderful to have seen all the things you've seen!

EMILIE. I've been employed in many houses, but what one sees does not change so very much, I've found.

HULDEY. I've never seen anything.

AGATHA. Mallory.

MARJORY. Yes ma'am.

AGATHA. Are you using the good teacups?

MARJORY. Yes ma'am.

AGATHA. And why is that.

MARJORY. Company, ma'am.

AGATHA. Miss Vandergaard is not company, Mallory. She's come to stay with us. She will be part of the family, now.

MARJORY. Yes ma'am.

AGATHA. That will be all.

*(**MARJORY** curtseys and leaves.)*

EMILIE. ...Was that not Marjory?

AGATHA. Marjory is the scullery maid.
Mallory is the parlor maid.

EMILIE. Yes...
But in actuality, was that not...?

*(**MARJORY** re-enters. Scullery maid hat.)*

AGATHA. What is it, Marjory.

MARJORY. I'm sent to inform you, the rest of the teacups have been broke, ma'am.

AGATHA. Broke?

MARJORY. Master Branwell...

AGATHA. Ah. Yes. I see.

MARJORY. That one time...

AGATHA. Yes yes. Nevermind. That will be all.

MARJORY. Yes ma'am.

(She exits. A beat.)

HULDEY. I'm sure there were lots of grand after-dinner diversions in the other houses? Games and parties and desserts perhaps?

EMILIE. I don't know...

HULDEY. What kinds of things did you do?

EMILIE. Nothing special... Sometimes I played a song or two, when the children asked.

HULDEY. What if you sang us a song now?

*(She looks at **AGATHA** hopefully. **EMILIE** tries to gauge **AGATHA**'s expression and fails.)*

EMILIE. Oh, I wouldn't like to impose...

HULDEY. She might play for us, Agatha, mightn't she?

EMILIE. It's just silliness, Huldey, your sister wouldn't want to be bothered with it.

*(A moment. **AGATHA** sizes her up. Then:)*

AGATHA. *(Cool.)* Why don't you play for us.

EMILIE. Are you sure?

AGATHA. In your letter to Master Branwell, you mentioned your particular love of music. I must imagine that you're quite good. Are you not quite good?

EMILIE. *(Flustered.)* Master Branwell mentioned that to you?

AGATHA. Are you good, or are you not good.

(A beat. **EMILIE** *meets* **AGATHA**'*s eyes. A little responding steeliness.)*

EMILIE. I'm fairly good.

AGATHA. Fairly?

EMILIE. I'm quite good.

AGATHA. I'll be the judge of that.

*(***HULDEY** *glances uneasily between them.)*

EMILIE. I should be delighted to oblige.

(She takes out her lute. She sings a song.)

(It's simple enough, but she's very good. It's strangely plaintive and haunting. It fills the space in a way that few things have filled it.)

(As she plays, **MARJORY** *sneaks back in and listens. The* **MASTIFF** *lifts his head.)*

(The song touches each of them in a way they didn't expect.)

[Cue: "Emilie's Song"]

WHEN I WAS A CHILD, I FELT AS A CHILD
WHEN I WAS A WOMAN, I FELT SOMETHING NEW
WHEN I BECOME OLD, I'LL TURN TO BONE OR HEATHER
WHEN I DIE THE WINDS WILL CRY BUT THE SKY WILL STILL BE BLUE.

WHEN YOU WERE A CHILD, YOU THOUGHT AS A CHILD
WHEN YOU WERE A WOMAN, YOU THOUGHT SOMETHING NEW
WHEN YOU BECOME OLD, YOU'LL CHANGE JUST LIKE THE WEATHER
WHEN YOU DIE THE WINDS WILL CRY BUT THE SUN WILL STILL SHINE THROUGH.

THERE'S A HAUNTING WIND ON THE MOORS TONIGHT
THERE'S A BLOOD RED MOON SO BOLD
THEY WILL ALL BUILD FIRES IN THE HEARTHS TONIGHT
BUT MINE ALONE STANDS COLD
THERE'S A BITING COLD IN THE AIR TONIGHT
BUT I ALONE DON'T MIND

OH FOR A LIFE WHERE WE'RE SIMPLE AS THE STARS
OH FOR A LIFE WHERE WE'RE FREER THAN THE GRASS
OH FOR A LIFE WHERE WE'RE BOLDER THAN THE DAYBREAK
AND OH FOR A LIFE WHERE, LIKE THE TIME, WE PASS.

(**EMILIE** *finishes her song.)*

(**MARJORY** *withdraws, unseen.)*

(**HULDEY** *is moved nearly to tears.* **AGATHA** *feels something stir inside her that's shocking and new. She pushes it down.)*

AGATHA. Well. That was passable.

EMILIE. It was quite good.

HULDEY. *(A dawning joy.)* It's so sad.

EMILIE. Would you like to sing, Miss Agatha?

AGATHA. No.

EMILIE. No?

AGATHA. Perish the thought.

HULDEY. *(Real pleasure.)* You made me feel...so sad.

EMILIE. Master Branwell says that there is nothing he enjoys more than a woman of many talents. Perhaps he might like to sing with us.

AGATHA. My brother had an eye for women, talented or otherwise.

EMILIE. I'm sure he means no harm by it.

AGATHA. Oh, are you sure?

(Slight beat.)

HULDEY. I've never made anybody feel as sad as that.

(Slight beat.)

EMILIE. Miss Agatha.

AGATHA. Yes.

EMILIE. In the past few hours since my arrival, have I given you any particular reason to dislike me?

(A real beat.)

AGATHA. Huldey. Would you be so kind.

HULDEY. What.

AGATHA. *(Indicating she should leave.) Would* you. Be. *So* kind.

*(**HULDEY** feels this rejection deeply.)*

*(She looks to **EMILIE** for help.)*

*(**EMILIE** doesn't say anything.)*

*(**HULDEY** feels the betrayal.)*

HULDEY. I had somewhere else to be anyway.

*(**HULDEY** leaves.)*

(A moment.)

AGATHA. Master Branwell is dead.

EMILIE. That is not possible.

AGATHA. Of course it is *possible*, child.
All things here are *possible*.

EMILIE. But I – From his very hand, I received –

AGATHA. Master Branwell suffered greatly from the typhus.
And then he passed.

EMILIE. But – the letter. All the letters.

AGATHA. Did you like them?

EMILIE. Did I...?

AGATHA. Did you enjoy them. Did you feel...generously toward their author.

EMILIE. They were very...affectionate letters.

AGATHA. They coaxed from you a warmth. Did they not. You responded in kind. Your affection grew.

EMILIE. When did Master Branwell pass?

AGATHA. Three months ago, give or take.

EMILIE. But…that cannot be possible, you see, for the letters –

AGATHA. They were by my hand.

(A beat.)

EMILIE. I don't believe you.

AGATHA. You think I cannot write…affectionately, when I choose?

EMILIE. That was not a woman's hand. A woman would not be capable of such letters.

AGATHA. I think, Miss Vandergaard, you know very little about women and what they are capable of. That is not your fault. You have been handed limitations, which you accepted. Perhaps accepting them *was* your fault. Either way, in your time here on the moors, perhaps you will become more knowledgeable.

(A beat.)

EMILIE. What am I doing here?

AGATHA. Pardon?

EMILIE. I came at the request of Master Branwell – yet I find he is dead. I'm here to look after a child – that I have not met, and that you seem in no hurry to have me meet. If I am not here for Master Branwell, or for the child, then what precisely is it for?

AGATHA. Do you wish to leave?

EMILIE. It was a question.

AGATHA. No one is a prisoner here, Emilie. If you are eager to return to London and seek yet another poorly paid position in yet another syphilitic household, you have only to repack your trunk.

EMILIE. It was only a question.

AGATHA. I didn't quite hear you.

EMILIE. I am not…eager.

AGATHA. Well then. More tea?

EMILIE. *Excuse* me?

AGATHA. Would you enjoy more tea?

Mallory!

(**MARJORY** *enters. Parlor hat. Curtseys. Tea.)*

AGATHA. My brother was a rageful man. So. There is that.
He broke the teacups. As you have heard.
Other things, too, were broken.
Dolls. When we were younger.
Eventually a neck or two.
He had his way with the maid, on multiple occasions.

EMILIE. With Marjory??

AGATHA. With Mallory.

EMILIE. But in actuality –?

AGATHA. Master Branwell was not a prudent man.

(A beat.)

EMILIE. Were *any* of the letters from Branwell?

AGATHA. Perhaps the first. What did the first say?

EMILIE. It notified me that my advertisement had come to his attention, and that his household was seeking a governess.

AGATHA. Oh. Yes. No. That was still myself.

EMILIE. And the...poetry? The...descriptions?

AGATHA. *(Can't help a little pride.)* You did like them, didn't you.

EMILIE. How can you sit there before me and admit to writing things of such a nature!

AGATHA. If they were badly written, that would be a different matter. None of what you received was badly written, don't you agree?

EMILIE. Badly written or not, it was shameless!

AGATHA. "Shameless."

EMILIE. A woman ought never –

AGATHA. A *woman*, Miss Vandergaard, desires results. A little girl desires approval, maybe. But a *woman* desires efficient results. I desired a governess. I wrote to one. She quit her immediate position and she came to me. Like a bee to a flower. Is that not... efficient? Is that not what you would call: a result?

(Beat.)

EMILIE. And now that I am here?

AGATHA. Now that you are here, you should rest. It's been quite a journey.

EMILIE. And your intentions? And the reason –?

AGATHA. You were right.

EMILIE. ...Excuse me?

AGATHA. Your song was more than passable.

(A beat between them.)

Mallory. Please show Miss Vandergaard to her bedroom.

MARJORY. Yes ma'am.

EMILIE. But...

AGATHA. Good night.

*(**AGATHA** stands. After a beat, **EMILIE** stands.)*

*(She follows **MARJORY** out.)*

*(The **MASTIFF** glances up at **AGATHA**.)*

Down.

*(**AGATHA** leaves the room as well.)*

5.

*(**HULDEY** sneaks in, diary in hand.)*

*(She addresses the **MASTIFF**.)*

HULDEY. Ah! You!

*(The **MASTIFF** looks at her dolefully. Re: her diary:)*

Oh, this?
Well if you insist, but just a little bit.
My diary is extremely private you see –
but since you ask so nicely –
but I have to warn you it is *very very* sad.

(She reads from her diary.)

Monday: I am very unhappy.
Tuesday: It is bleak here, and I am unhappy.
Wednesday: There was fog, and my digestive system was disagreeable, and I was greatly unhappy.
Thursday: There is a driving rain on the moors, and a governess arrived, she has beautiful hair and when she says my name it sounds like a song that was written just for me. I think we shall be best friends, closer than sisters.

(A new feeling, in the moment:)

Friday: The governess does not seem to keep a diary.

*(Beat. She looks at the **MASTIFF**. He looks back.)*

It's hard to be rather well-known. I wouldn't say *famous* – but someone else might. Whenever I go to the village, everybody says, "There is the parson's youngest daughter." They say, "I wonder what exciting thing she is thinking today!" They say, "I hear she's a famous writer." And one doesn't like to be talked about all the time, it makes one feel quite uncomfortable, so I say, "Oh stop, I'm just like you, there's nothing special about me at all." And they just *refuse* to believe me. They think I'm special. They think it's so very evident, when they look at me, that I was destined for wonderful things, even if I can't see those things myself, it's so very evident to every last one of them.

(Beat. **HULDEY** *bursts into tears.)*

(The **MASTIFF** *takes a deep breath.)*

(He tries to communicate to **HULDEY** *in her preferred medium.)*

MASTIFF. Monday.

I met God.

He was a moor-hen, and He fled from me.

Was I supposed to pursue?

HULDEY. *(Hearing none of this – crossly.)* Oh just go away. Big awful dog. Snuffling on everything. I hate it here. I hate everything. I hate you.

(She throws her diary at him.)

(The **MASTIFF** *sighs and leaves.)*

6.

(The **MOOR-HEN** *sits, leg at a bad angle.)*

(The **MASTIFF** *approaches.)*

MASTIFF. Hello.

MOOR-HEN. Aaaah!

MASTIFF. It's just me.

MOOR-HEN. Have we met?

MASTIFF. Yes! You fell from the sky. You dislike flying. I asked you about God.

MOOR-HEN. Oh! Yes. You were difficult. To understand. But not disagreeable.

MASTIFF. Thank you.

MOOR-HEN. But uncomfortably large.

MASTIFF. What's wrong with your leg?

MOOR-HEN. Crash-landing.

MASTIFF. That looks painful.

MOOR-HEN. It isn't the most fun I've ever had.

MASTIFF. Do you need help?

MOOR-HEN. What help! You stay over there.

MASTIFF. Good help. Non-violent help.

MOOR-HEN. Unless you can grow me another leg, I don't see how you'd help.

MASTIFF. I could set your leg at a better angle.
I could make you soup.

MOOR-HEN. Why would you do any of those things.

MASTIFF. I want us to talk.

MOOR-HEN. Why?

MASTIFF. *(Faster and faster.)* Because nobody ever talks to me, and I never talk to anybody.
And I have so many thoughts.
I stay up late at night. With all my thoughts.
They echo around inside my head.

Until it gets so everything seems terrible and sharp-edged and awful.

I can't remember that there was ever anything good at all.

And people look at my face. They look at my face and they see nothing.

They think there are no expressions on my face, just because they don't know how to look for the expressions that *are* on my face.

They think I'm guarded. But actually, if anybody truly *asked* me anything, I would tell them! I don't want to be all alone with my thoughts! It's like being in a dark room all the time and you don't have any hands and nobody thinks to open the door for you!

(Deep breath.)

Sorry.

I'm sorry.

I didn't mean to say all of that.

I'm just not used to anybody listening.

MOOR-HEN. How do you know I'm listening?

MASTIFF. You might not be, but you're sitting still and looking at me, and that's good enough.

(Beat.)

(He approaches. This time, she lets him get pretty close. And then stops him.)

MOOR-HEN. That's close enough.

MASTIFF. I've been thinking about you a lot.

MOOR-HEN. *(A little flattered, also alarmed.)* Have you?

MASTIFF. I addressed God, and then there you were. It can't be a coincidence.

MOOR-HEN. Look, I don't know what a coincidence is, but sometimes things just happen, you know?

MASTIFF. That's called a coincidence.

MOOR-HEN. Oh!

(Beat.)

MASTIFF. But I've just been talking about me. I want to know about you.

If flying doesn't make you happy, why do you do it?

MOOR-HEN. Happy?

MASTIFF. We talked about this.

MOOR-HEN. I have a terrible memory. It's why I never really learn new things. But also, I don't worry all that much, so it works for me, in a limited way.

MASTIFF. It's this clench-knot – nevermind.

Tell me about flying.

MOOR-HEN. Well. When I'm up, I'm up and up and up!

...And then I'm DOWN.

And then usually something hurts.

And this time, something hurts a lot.

MASTIFF. Are you sure you don't want me to take a look at it?

MOOR-HEN. You just stay right where you are.

MASTIFF. I used to imagine that if I could fly, it would make me happy.

To just...from high above, look down at things.

I imagine that if you can see the parameters of things, you can love them. I imagine that's why God loves everybody. And also because he doesn't actually have to be touched by us.

MOOR-HEN. I've been up there. It's not that great.

MASTIFF. Oh.

(Beat.)

MOOR-HEN. Look.

MASTIFF. Yes?

MOOR-HEN. You look like a squashed grub. Like a little flat grub with its insides coming out of its outsides.

MASTIFF. I'm depressed.

MOOR-HEN. I don't know what that is.

MASTIFF. It's a little flat grub with its insides coming out of its outsides.

MOOR-HEN. Shouldn't you do something about that?

MASTIFF. I'm talking to you.

MOOR-HEN. Oh.

And are you feeling less..."depressed"?

MASTIFF. I think so, yes.

MOOR-HEN. *(Baffled, flattered.)* Oh!

(Beat. It starts to rain.)

Great. Just great.

This day sucks.

MASTIFF. Can I come closer?

MOOR-HEN. Why?

MASTIFF. Because I am very big and you are very small and it's raining, and if I stand over you, I will get all the rain, and none of it will reach you.

MOOR-HEN. Oh.

Well.

Hmm.

MASTIFF. And I won't eat you at all.

MOOR-HEN. Well okay but just this time.

(The **MASTIFF** *walks to the* **MOOR-HEN.***)*

(He shields her from the rain.)

(It's intimate and amazing and terrifying.)

MOOR-HEN. Are you cold?

MASTIFF. No.

MOOR-HEN. You're shaking.

MASTIFF. I've never been this close to someone.

MOOR-HEN. That can't be true.

MASTIFF. I've never been this close to someone who was actually looking at me.

MOOR-HEN. I can close my eyes.

MASTIFF. No! No.

Don't close your eyes.
Please.

MOOR-HEN. Okay then.

MASTIFF. I have the strangest…sensation.

MOOR-HEN. Is it the typhus?

MASTIFF. It's this feeling
in my heart-cavern
as if spring has come
and all the birds are falling upwards.

(They stand. It rains.)

(The **MASTIFF** *falls in love.)*

7.

(**MARJORY** *polishes shiny things in the scullery.*)

(**EMILIE** *appears in the doorway.*)

EMILIE. There you are!

(**MARJORY** *is startled.*)

I didn't mean to startle you.

MARJORY. I'm not startled.

EMILIE. Are you Marjory or Mallory right now?

MARJORY. I'm in the scullery, so I'm the scullery maid.

EMILIE. ...Is this the scullery?

MARJORY. What does it look like.

(*A beat. Let's not answer this.*)

(**EMILIE** *zeroes in on* **MARJORY.**)

EMILIE. Yes-typhus, no-baby?

MARJORY. Very good.

EMILIE. How's the baby?

MARJORY. Unwanted.

EMILIE. Which is preferable, typhus or a child?

MARJORY. Well, neither is preferable.

EMILIE. You have a point.

MARJORY. Which is preferable, being a governess in London, or being a governess here?

EMILIE. London, probably. Maybe not.

MARJORY. Which is preferable, being eaten by wolves, or being a governess?

EMILIE. Is that a joke?

MARJORY. Did you find it funny?

EMILIE. Not particularly.

MARJORY. Then it wasn't a joke.

(*Beat.*)

EMILIE. You knew that Master Branwell was dead, and you didn't say a word to me.

MARJORY. I don't know anything.

EMILIE. He's been dead three months.

MARJORY. If you say so.

EMILIE. *(Alarmed.)* Is he dead or isn't he?

MARJORY. He's whatever Mistress Agatha says he is.

EMILIE. I don't like that answer at all.

MARJORY. I have to go polish things.

EMILIE. You just keep on polishing. Right here.

MARJORY. No, I have to go to a place where you aren't, and polish things.

(Beat.)

EMILIE. Do you like sweets? I'll give you a sweet.

MARJORY. God doesn't like sweet things.

EMILIE. Or a pretty piece of lace. I have some pretty lace I brought all the way from London.

MARJORY. God doesn't like pretty things either.

EMILIE. What do you want?

(Beat.)

MARJORY. You do this.

EMILIE. What?

*(**MARJORY** hands her the polishing cloth.)*

MARJORY. You.

*(Beat. **EMILIE** laughs. **MARJORY** doesn't.)*

*(Beat. **EMILIE** takes the cloth.)*

(Beat.)

Go on.

EMILIE. I – what do I –?

MARJORY. You scrub.

EMILIE. *(Laughing.)* This is really rather...

MARJORY. God loves women. On their knees. Scrubbing.

*(Beat. **EMILIE** sees **MARJORY** isn't kidding.)*

*(Beat. **EMILY** tentatively polishes.)*

Harder.

(Scrubs harder.)

Harder.

(Scrubs harder.)

Harder than that.

*(***EMILIE*** scrubs harder than that.)*

*(***MARJORY*** watches, no expression on her face.)*

EMILIE. *(Scrubbing.)* Is Branwell dead or alive?

MARJORY. You have to put your back into it.

EMILIE. *(Putting her back into it.)* And where is the child I'm to watch? I've been here two days already.

MARJORY. You're not doing it right.

EMILIE. *(Frustrated.)* How am I not doing it right!

MARJORY. You'd do it better if you had the typhus, I think.

EMILIE. This is all a little much.

MARJORY. Come closer.

EMILIE. What.

*(***MARJORY*** leans forward and coughs in* ***EMILIE****'s face.* ***EMILIE*** *steps back, shocked.)*

MARJORY. There you go.

Now scrub.

EMILIE. Now look here –!

MARJORY. Master Branwell is living in the attic. If you want to call that "living."

You want more? Scrub like you mean it.

(A shocked beat. ***EMILIE*** *does want more.)*

(She scrubs again.)

EMILIE. Whatever is he doing in the attic?

MARJORY. You'd scrub better if you were pregnant, I think. Come here.

EMILIE. *(Completely alarmed.)* No!

MARJORY. Do you want to know what it is to scrub well, or don't you?

EMILIE. Why is he in the attic!

MARJORY. Before she laid the last brick. There was a small ray of light coming through the brick wall, where the hole was, and he put his face to it. He could barely reach, because of the chains. But he put his mouth to it as if he could drink the sunlight. He said: "Don't do this." But he knew she would do it, of course.

EMILIE. Who? Who would do such a thing?

(**MARJORY** *approaches her, with a cold stare.*)

(It's utterly disconcerting.)

MARJORY. Close your eyes.

EMILIE. I don't want to.

MARJORY. But I didn't ask. What you wanted.
I didn't ask that.

EMILIE. *(Backed into a corner.)* I want to go home.

MARJORY. This is your home, isn't it? This is your home now.

(**AGATHA** *enters.*)

AGATHA. Mallory.

MARJORY. *(Immediately transformed.)* Yes ma'am.

AGATHA. What *are* you doing.

MARJORY. Showing Miss Vandergaard the...scullery, ma'am.

AGATHA. She does not need to see it.

MARJORY. Yes ma'am.

AGATHA. You are a very idle girl, Marjory. Go and make yourself useful elsewhere.

MARJORY. Yes ma'am.

(**MARJORY** *exits.*)

(A beat between **AGATHA** *and* **EMILIE.***)*

AGATHA. Did she upset you?

EMILIE. *(Very upset.)* Not at all.

AGATHA. You seem as if you might cry.

EMILIE. I don't believe in crying.

*(***AGATHA*** takes* **EMILIE** *in, with grudging respect. The thing she felt during the song flickers for her again.)*

AGATHA. ...Perhaps you would like to take a walk.

EMILIE. A walk?

AGATHA. We have some matters to discuss. Where better to do so than on the moors. The fresh air. The daylight. The brisk wind.

EMILIE. And the quicksand? And the ravenous birds?

AGATHA. You shall enjoy it all immensely.

(And as they move, the whole world transforms...)

8.

(The moors. **AGATHA** *and* **EMILIE.***)*

(The skies go on forever.)

(The light is hypnotic and terrifying and beautiful.)

AGATHA. What do you think?

EMILIE. It's rather...large.

AGATHA. Yes.

EMILIE. And cold.

AGATHA. Yes.

EMILIE. One might get lost out here, so easily.

AGATHA. One wrong turn and it's all over.

EMILIE. I don't even know where the house is.

AGATHA. One might look around in all directions and see no sign of civilization whatsoever.

(Beat.)

EMILIE. Does it not seem very lonely to you?

AGATHA. It does.

EMILIE. And does it not make you dreadfully sad?

AGATHA. I find it comforting.

EMILIE. Comforting?

AGATHA. I cannot stand weakness. I cannot stand it in myself, and I cannot abide it in others.

There is no weakness in the moors.

When I come out here, I am surrounded by merciless strength.

EMILIE. But mightn't it turn on you? Mightn't you be devoured by it?

AGATHA. Yes, absolutely.

(A beat. **EMILIE** *is impressed despite herself.)*

EMILIE. The maid says you bricked Master Branwell in the attic.

AGATHA. Which maid was it?

EMILIE. Marjory.
Mallory.
Is it untrue?

AGATHA. No, no. All true.

EMILIE. That's horrible!

AGATHA. *(A real question.)* Why is it horrible?

*(**EMILIE** thinks about this.)*

EMILIE. Well. He was your brother.

AGATHA. He gambled. He deflowered virgins. He ran up considerable debts.

EMILIE. So you chose to punish him for his ungodly ways?

AGATHA. Oh. No. One gets tired of cleaning up after others. And then one wishes to be rid of them.

EMILIE. That's it?

AGATHA. After father died, Branwell's indiscretions made life particularly irritating. Life became much less irritating when Branwell was in the attic.

EMILIE. Is he dead?

AGATHA. I left him with a loaf of bread.
Of course, one loaf of bread does not last for three months.

(Beat.)

EMILIE. *(This isn't a bad thing.)* You are very heartless and cruel.

AGATHA. No. You see, that is a common fallacy. That strength on the part of humans is cruelty. Here upon the moors, do you think one is coddled? No. A bird or a fox or a dragon-fly, it must survive from sheer strength and will alone. And does one call the moors "cruel"? "Heartless"? No. One accepts them for what they are. Inhospitable, perhaps. But that is their nature. One accepts that nature – and only by accepting, nay, embracing it, can one truly be at home here.

EMILIE. You are unlike anyone I have ever met.

AGATHA. And what do you make of it?

(Beat. The spark between them intensifies.)

EMILIE. Did you truly write those letters?

AGATHA. I did.

EMILIE. And you read my letters.

AGATHA. Of course.

EMILIE. Did you read them in the parlor? Or did you wait until you were in your bedchamber?

AGATHA. Oh, I chose the privacy of my bedchamber.

EMILIE. *(Shy.)* And did they...delight you?

AGATHA. I found them very instructive.

EMILIE. Instructive...?

AGATHA. I found them quite telling. I read into them a great deal about your character, and its weaknesses, and how easily you find yourself at the mercy of the world.

EMILIE. *(Bold.)* But pleasure, Agatha. Did you find in them any...pleasure?

*(**AGATHA** sizes her up. **AGATHA** smiles.)*

AGATHA. Have you ever had a love affair, little Emilie?

EMILIE. One doesn't talk about such things.

AGATHA. One doesn't. You're right. One does not.
But here we are, and we are entirely alone...

EMILIE. When I – when I read his letters – your letters – they made me strangely – warm.

AGATHA. Did they.

EMILIE. A sort of a...pins and needles feeling. In all my extremities. Even my toes.

AGATHA. And did you like it?

EMILIE. Oh, it was very dangerous.

AGATHA. Did *you* take these letters to bed with you? Did you sleep with them against your skin?

EMILIE. I might have.

AGATHA. And you did it so you could dream of him.

EMILIE. I – yes, maybe I did.

AGATHA. And you did, you did dream of me, and it was very nice. Wasn't it.

EMILIE. It was.

AGATHA. In your dream you came to this house. And that first night at the dinner table, he had eyes only for you.

EMILIE. He stared at me with bright, dark eyes. He saw me.

AGATHA. And you were seen, as you had never before been seen.

EMILIE. And days passed, of course. One doesn't move too quickly.

AGATHA. And then one night I came to your room, I stood in your door.

EMILIE. It was a dark night, only the hint of a moon.

AGATHA. And the roughness of my stubble against your palm.

EMILIE. Against my cheek.

(**AGATHA** *touches her cheek.*)

AGATHA. The roughness of my hands.

EMILIE. And everything so dark, it's hard to see –

AGATHA. – and no time to stop...

EMILIE. And I did not wish to.

AGATHA. You did not wish to stop.

(**AGATHA** *kisses* **EMILIE. EMILIE** *could live in that kiss, but eventually* **AGATHA** *breaks it.*)

You asked why I brought you here.

EMILY. It doesn't matter.

AGATHA. Of course it matters.

I have brought you here to claim greatness.

EMILY. Greatness?

AGATHA. My sister, as you have seen, is worthless.

My brother was worse.

The maid is beyond hope.

But you...you will obey me, little Emilie.

EMILIE. I...will?

AGATHA. With great precision and determination and unswerving loyalty.

You will do so because, for the first time in your short and unremarkable life, you have been chosen. Above others, over others. You, and only you.

EMILIE. Did you really consider others?

AGATHA. I did.

EMILIE. *(This means a lot to her.)* ...Oh.

AGATHA. Master Branwell is in the attic. As you know.

What you do not know is this: While he may be close to death, he is not yet dead.

Marjory brings him a thin gruel, to keep him on this side of life.

She moves aside the final brick, as it has not yet been mortared, and she pours that thin gruel through the hole and into his weak and waiting mouth.

EMILIE. Why have you chosen to keep him alive?

AGATHA. When you have a child, it will be my child. And when we are all dead, that child will remain. And our family will live forever.

EMILIE. When *I* have...?

AGATHA. And that is Master Branwell's purpose.

9.

*(**HULDEY** and her diary. In the library...which is the same as the parlor. The moor-rain continues.)*

HULDEY. *(A rush of anguish.)* Monday: Agatha is awful, Emilie only ever talks to her, yesterday they went on a walk, upon returning from the walk, Emilie didn't even seem to *notice* that I was in the room, Emilie is uglier than I initially thought she was, and I hate Agatha.

(A breath.)

Tuesday: I think I'm going to kill myself.

Wednesday: If I killed myself, nobody would even notice.

Thursday –

*(**MARJORY** enters without a hat.)*

MARJORY. Oh. Pardon.

HULDEY. Mallory!

MARJORY. Ma'am.

HULDEY. Marjory?

MARJORY. Ma'am.

HULDEY. You've been lurking outside the Library to hear my innermost private thoughts!

MARJORY. Oh no, not at –

HULDEY. It's all right, everyone does it, sit down and I'll read to you.

(Reading.)

Thurs–

MARJORY. I'll just go and take care of the...

HULDEY. No! You sit there. You sit right there.

"Thursday: I had a dream about a great hulking awful man who came into my bedchamber. I was terrified and it was terrible and I did not want him in my bedchamber AT. ALL. And we talked for a very long time."

(To **MARJORY.***)*

You come here. Come here.

MARJORY. I'm feeling labor pains, ma'am, I think I should sit.

HULDEY. No come here. You are going to read the part of the awful man, and I am going to read the part of me, in my lacy nightgown.

MARJORY. And also my typhus is acting up again, I've been coughing blood all morning.

HULDEY. Come here RIGHT NOW.

*(***MARJORY** *goes to her.* **HULDEY** *reads.)*

HULDEY-AS-HEROINE. "What can you possibly want with me, you awful man."

MARJORY-AS-AWFUL-MAN. *(Flat monotone.)* "I cannot keep away from you."

HULDEY-AS-HEROINE. "What nonsense. How horrible. What are you doing."

MARJORY-AS-AWFUL-MAN. *(Flat monotone.)* "I am worshipping you with my eyes."

HULDEY-AS-HEROINE. "That is very obscene and uncalled-for. What are you doing now?"

MARJORY-AS-AWFUL-MAN. *(Flat monotone.)* "I am worshipping you with more than my eyes."

(Beat – as herself.)

Ma'am?

HULDEY. What is it.

MARJORY. *(Trying to leave.)* I really have to –

HULDEY-AS-HEROINE. *(Steam-rolling over her.)* "How brutal! How ravishing! God can see us and is judging you!"

MARJORY-AS-AWFUL-MAN. *(Flat monotone.)* "I have loved you long before you were as famous as you are currently famous. I have always wanted to know your innermost thoughts and emotions."

HULDEY-AS-HEROINE. "Really?"

MARJORY-AS-AWFUL-MAN. *(Flat monotone.)* "Quite sincerely."

HULDEY-AS-HEROINE. "Well. What would you like to know?"

MARJORY. *(As herself.)* Why don't you kill Agatha?

(A bewildered beat.)

*(**HULDEY** stares at her.)*

HULDEY-AS-HEROINE. "Excuse me?"

MARJORY. *(As herself.)* I said:
Why don't you kill Agatha?

*(A beat. **HULDEY** is completely off-balanced.)*

HULDEY. Kill. Agatha?
I...
Kill? Agatha?

MARJORY. You'd be the sister who killed her sister.
A woman murderess.
The parson's daughter!
It would be shocking and horrible and nobody would be able to stop talking about it.
You'd be infamous.

HULDEY. *(Trying the word out.)* *"IN*...famous."

MARJORY. It's like famous. But moreso.

HULDEY. I know what the word means. I'm an author.

MARJORY. Also, you might write about it.
What it was like to kill Agatha.
How you felt about it, before and after.

HULDEY. People always do seem to want to know those things.

MARJORY. They might want to ask you themselves.
They might want to come up here and ask you.

HULDEY. And I of course should feel very strongly about my privacy, and wouldn't want any of that sort of vulgar crowd in my parlor. Drinking my tea and asking me such intimate questions.

(Dreaming a little.)

HULDEY. How I feel. What it all means. Where I think I'm going in my life next, and do I think it was because I lacked love as a child, which of course is true, I *did* lack love as a child, what an astute question.

MARJORY. That *is*. That *is* an astute question.

HULDEY. *(Carried away by all of this.)* Did *you* lack love as a child?

MARJORY. I did, I really did.

HULDEY. Everything around here is so bleak. So loveless and bleak. And if I were to kill Agatha – and I'm not saying I would, of course – but if I *were*, it would sort of be a...splash of color. If you will. A tear in the fabric.

MARJORY. Wrenching control of your life.

Of *history*.

HULDEY. *History?*

MARJORY. A new chapter unrolling before your eyes.

Monday: today everything changed.

HULDEY. Monday: Everything was gray and cold and then all of a sudden – BAM!

MARJORY. Monday: "Bam."

HULDEY. *(A revelation!)* They might write a song about it!

MARJORY. Sorry?

HULDEY. There are all sorts of ballads about that kind of thing.

They might write a ballad about me.

MARJORY. They might. They would.

HULDEY. Maybe if I sort of wrote my own ballad about it, that might be the one they ended up singing all the time. So it would be like, I'd be famous as a writer and a murderer but *also* as sort of a singer-songwriter.

MARJORY. That sounds very likely.

*(***HULDEY** *hugs her impulsively.* **MARJORY** *stands very still.)*

HULDEY. This is the best day I've ever had.

10.

(The moors.)

(The **MASTIFF** *and the* **MOOR-HEN.***)*

(She eats. He guards her. He's never been so at peace in the world. Mid-conversation.)

MASTIFF. ...But then sometimes I think, who would I be if I weren't depressed?

You know?

As if the thing that is making me myself is my own constant and unyielding misery. As if happiness is some sort of altered state, in which you're no longer quite yourself.

MOOR-HEN. What's "depressed" again?

MASTIFF. The squashed grub.

MOOR-HEN. Oh! That's right.

Why do you want to be a squashed grub again?

MASTIFF. Forget it.

MOOR-HEN. Say it again slower.

MASTIFF. You know, it actually doesn't matter.

MOOR-HEN. It doesn't?

MASTIFF. You're here now, so it doesn't.

MOOR-HEN. That's nice.

(Reflective beat.)

Is that nice?

MASTIFF. It's nice.

MOOR-HEN. Okay.

(Beat.)

MASTIFF. How's your leg?

MOOR-HEN. Still hurts.

MASTIFF. Are you sure you don't want some soup? Or a blanket?

MOOR-HEN. I'm fine.

MASTIFF. Or something sweet?
Or I could pick you some flowers.

MOOR-HEN. I'm perfectly fine.

MASTIFF. Or I could make you a bed out of hay and you could sleep in it.

MOOR-HEN. I'm okay. But thank you.

MASTIFF. I just want to help. I want to do things for you.

MOOR-HEN. You're already helping.

MASTIFF. Am I?

MOOR-HEN. Well, nothing has tried to eat me while you've been here.

MASTIFF. Well that's true.

(Beat.)

MOOR-HEN. Why do you want to do things for me?

MASTIFF. You make me feel good.

MOOR-HEN. You told me you feel like a grub.

MASTIFF. No, that's all the times that I'm not with you.
When I'm with you, I feel like the sky is much smaller, or else I'm much bigger, and all the things that were ready to swallow me are now possibly weaker than I am.

MOOR-HEN. *(Shy.)* When I'm with you...

(She stops.)

MASTIFF. What?
No what, say it.

MOOR-HEN. It's dumb.

MASTIFF. No it's not!

MOOR-HEN. You don't even know what I was going to say.

MASTIFF. It's not dumb.
Come on.

MOOR-HEN. I was just going to say...that when I'm with you...
I can't.

MASTIFF. You can!

(They're both laughing.)

MOOR-HEN. This is so stupid.

MASTIFF. I won't look at you.

MOOR-HEN. Okay don't look.

(He looks away – in a rush:)

When I'm with you I feel like the space between taking off and landing. The sort of rush. The part before everything hurts.

MASTIFF. *(Very soberly.)* Do you really feel like that?

MOOR-HEN. I do.

MASTIFF. That makes me really happy.

That makes me feel like something I don't know how to describe.

MOOR-HEN. *(Gently.)* It's not forever though.

MASTIFF. What do you mean?

MOOR-HEN. It's just for now. Right?

MASTIFF. What are you talking about?

MOOR-HEN. Everything is a season. The rains are a season and the cold is a season and the heat is a very short season. Everything happens and then something else happens.

MASTIFF. The way I feel about you is not a "something else happens." It's an always.

MOOR-HEN. Listen.

You're wonderful.

But you're a very large dog, and your diet generally consists of...well. Things like me. And I know I'm not incredibly intelligent, and my short-term memory is – well. Short – But I don't really see this ending well.

MASTIFF. I would never ever hurt you.

MOOR-HEN. Every time I get up into the air, there's a moment in which all I feel is the wind rushing past me. It's very exciting and it feels very good. And I believe that it is good. But even though I intend to stay UP UP UP, the DOWN always hits eventually.

MASTIFF. This isn't like that at all.

MOOR-HEN. All I mean is...

MASTIFF. *(Upset.)* This isn't gravity, this is love!

MOOR-HEN. Okay.

MASTIFF. Okay?

MOOR-HEN. Forget it.

(Beat.)

MASTIFF. I'll get you some hay. I'll make you a nest. And I'll take care of you. And even if it rains, you'll never get wet, and when the moor-wind blows, you'll never be cold, and I will stand over you and we will be so happy. Okay?

MOOR-HEN. I guess so.

11.

*(**MARJORY** in the Portrait Gallery...which is the same room as the parlor.)*

(She sits in the good chair. Feet up.)

(She is not polishing anything.)

*(She writes in **HULDEY**'s diary.)*

MARJORY. Monday: I polished.

Tuesday: I polished and I cooked.

Wednesday: I cooked more things and afterwards I scrubbed.

Thursday: It rained and Miss Emilie tracked mud everywhere and I cleaned it.

Friday: I told Huldey to murder Miss Agatha.

(Musing.)

I should like to be in charge. Why should everybody else have a say but me? *I'm* the one with ideas. And my diary is full of action verbs. And if people were to ask me questions, I should have a lot more to say for myself, because I've done a lot more, I've considered a lot more, and I have a lot of thoughts about the moors and manual labor and the typhus, and also child-rearing, and if Huldey does not kill Miss Agatha soon, I shall have to murder them both, although I would much prefer someone else to do it.

*(**HULDEY** enters.)*

(There is a different air about her.)

(The air of a woman heading toward greatness.)

HULDEY. There you are! I've been looking for you.

MARJORY. I've been here, in the Portrait Gallery.

HULDEY. Aren't you supposed to be...scrubbing? Something?

MARJORY. Every good murderess needs a confidante and a chronicler. So right now, I am confidanting and chronicling.

HULDEY. Is that my diary?

MARJORY. No, right now this is An Historical Record. Multiple voices go into making up An Historical Record.

HULDEY. Multiple?

MARJORY. First yours. And now mine.

HULDEY. Hm.

(Beat – on to more exciting things!)

I've been working on my ballad!

MARJORY. Your what?

HULDEY. The ballad about killing Agatha.

MARJORY. ...But you haven't killed her yet.

HULDEY. No, I want the ballad ready for when I do.

MARJORY. Don't you think you should be focusing on the murder?

HULDEY. I want everything ready for when it happens. I want the ballad ready, so nobody else tries to stick their own stupid ballad in its place, and I want to pick out the right outfit and I haven't done that yet.

MARJORY. But how are you going to kill her?

(A beat. **HULDEY** *has not considered this.)*

HULDEY. Well, I don't know. I mean. People die out here all the time.

MARJORY. People *die*, but people are not *murdered.*

HULDEY. I mean there's...exposure. Isn't there? The typhus? Complications?

MARJORY. Your sister is not ailing in the slightest.

HULDEY. Perhaps I might...uh...lure her out into the moors! "Agatha," I might say, "come outside at once!" And then she will get lost and the quicksand will suck her under and that will be that.

(Oh dear, this could all be going terribly awry. But **MARJORY** *rallies.)*

MARJORY. *(Crafty.)* You can't put that in a ballad.

HULDEY. No?

MARJORY. No! If you're going to write a good ballad, you need a good murder, which involves an axe or a pick or a dagger or at the very least poison.

HULDEY. You've thought about this.

MARJORY. You haven't!

HULDEY. I have!

I have all my answers ready for when people interview me and ask me lots of questions.

MARJORY. You have *answers*?

HULDEY. Interview me! Go on! Ask me, "Huldeygard, why did you murder your elder sister in such callous and cold blood."

MARJORY. "Huldeygard, why did you –"

HULDEY. I was a woman pushed to desperate straits, I tell you, desperate! Here on the moors one reaches such extremity of emotion! Now, of course, I see the error of my ways and I repent.

MARJORY. That's no good at all.

HULDEY. *(Crushed.)* I thought it was rather good.

MARJORY. You can't repent! You can't see the error of your ways!

HULDEY. I can't?

MARJORY. It's BORING.

HULDEY. ...Oh.

MARJORY. Nobody CARES about people who are SORRY.

Everybody FORGETS the people who are SORRY.

The only people who get remembered are the ones who are NEVER SORRY.

*(**HULDEY** takes this in. Way in.)*

HULDEY. Wow.

MARJORY. Just forget it. You weren't cut out for this.

HULDEY. No! No wait.

MARJORY. I have to go scrub something.

HULDEY. No wait! I can be. I can be cut out for this.

MARJORY. I don't think so. You want to be sorry and you want to be forgiven.

HULDEY. I can not want those things! I can be very cold and very brutal.

MARJORY. Can you?

HULDEY. Interview me again.

MARJORY. "Huldeygard, why did you murder your elder sister in such callous and cold blood."

HULDEY. *(Coldly and with poise.)* Because that is what I am, sir. A murderess.

(Beat. Okay. Better.)

MARJORY. "And how do you feel in the aftermath?"

HULDEY. Nothing.

MARJORY. "Nothing?"

HULDEY. I feel nothing.

(Beat.)

MARJORY. That was okay.

HULDEY. Was it good?

MARJORY. It was better.

HULDEY. It was good, wasn't it.

MARJORY. You *are* going to do it, aren't you?

HULDEY. Of course.

MARJORY. Of course?

HULDEY. Of course I'm going to do it!

MARJORY. Okay.
When?

HULDEY. What?

MARJORY. I said: When. Are you going to do it?

(Beat.)

HULDEY. Well. Soon.

(Beat.)

MARJORY. Someone else might do it first. If you didn't.

HULDEY. What?!

MARJORY. I'm just saying. It's an opportunity. Everybody wants opportunity. So if you didn't take this one, someone else might do it, and then you wouldn't be anything, really. You'd just be sad old Huldey alone in the house on the moors. Sad sad Huldey, whose sister got killed by someone else, which would get you a little pity, I guess, a sympathy-vote, but nobody likes to think about victims, it makes them feel sad, so eventually nobody would like to think about you. At all. Ever.

(A beat. **HULDEY** *stands with newfound conviction.)*

HULDEY. Nobody is going to murder my sister before I do.

(She marches from the room.)

*(***MARJORY** *watches her go.)*

12.

*(**AGATHA**'s bedchamber. Which appears to be the same room as the parlor.* **AGATHA** *sits in a very uncomfortable chair. She reads* **EMILIE**'s *letters to herself.)*

AGATHA. Ah.

(Reads.)

Yes.

(Reads – corrects the spelling.)

With an "A," Emilie, not an "I."

(Reads.)

Not bad.

(At a sound nearby:)

Yes?

*(**EMILIE** steps into the light.)*

EMILIE. May I?

AGATHA. It is very late. It is very late to be slipping into people's bedrooms.

EMILIE. I know.

AGATHA. Come in.

*(**EMILIE** does. Looking around.)*

EMILIE. Your bedroom is very...spare.

AGATHA. Yes.

Will you have a nightcap?

EMILIE. *(A little shocked.)* Do you drink?

AGATHA. Do you find it unladylike?

EMILIE. Of course.

AGATHA. Good.

(She produces a flask. Offers it. **EMILIE** *takes it and sips. Then returns to* **AGATHA**.*)*

So...why have you come at this hour?

EMILIE. I had to see you.

AGATHA. *(But gently.)* Impulse is not the same thing as courage.

EMILIE. Neither is liquor.

AGATHA. *(Toasting slightly.)* A fair point.

(A beat.)

EMILIE. I have thought about it. What you're asking.

It would once have been unthinkable.

AGATHA. But now it is not?

EMILIE. When we were out on the moors...everything was... endless. And some might call it unforgiving. Bleak. Terrifying, even. My eyes saw it that way at first. But as we stood there I began to see it as you did. As a place of...power, perhaps. A place that belonged to itself. And I wondered...what it would be, to belong to a place like that.

AGATHA. Did you.

EMILIE. I've moved from house to house my whole life. There's always a lady of the house who can't abide me, a gentleman of the house who pursues me, a child who dies of something awful – and then I move on. Wherever I go, it is all the same, and I'm always a stranger. What you showed me...it has a strong pull.

AGATHA. "However"?

EMILIE. However.

A young girl, unprotected, requires certain assurances.

AGATHA. *(Surprised and interested.)* "Assurances."

EMILIE. You understand.

AGATHA. We'll see if I do. Go on.

EMILIE. My child will be the heir to all of this. Is that not right?

AGATHA. *My* child.

EMILIE. ...*Our* child.

AGATHA. *(Acknowledges: term one.)* ...will be the heir, yes.

EMILIE. And this child will need a firm and guiding hand. From its mother, who must be nearby.

AGATHA. "Nearby"?

EMILIE. *(Direct.)* My own wing and my own servant.

AGATHA. One room, near the nursery. Mallory will be your servant.

EMILIE. My own wing, and Mallory won't do.

AGATHA. Two rooms, in the west wing. Mallory will be instructed to behave better toward you.

EMILIE. Two rooms, in perpetuity. I can handle Mallory myself.

AGATHA. In *perpetuity*?

EMILIE. If I give this family an heir, I give it life. By my calculation, that makes me a member.

(A beat, and then **AGATHA** *smiles.)*

AGATHA. I am so rarely surprised. But how enjoyable when it occurs.

EMILIE. ...Thank you.

AGATHA. I have chosen well, and you will perform satisfactorily, and that makes me...content.

EMILIE. I'd like to make you happy.

AGATHA. I believe the word I used was "content."
Well. Shall we shake on it?

(Beat.)

EMILIE. And then there is the matter of...what lies between us.

AGATHA. Excuse me?

EMILIE. Have I surprised you again?

AGATHA. Twice is one night is a little much.

EMILIE. I see the way you look at me. And when you see that I see, and you become cold – that doesn't escape my notice either.

AGATHA. I can't imagine what you're referring to.

EMILIE. You wanted a sweet young governess and you summoned one, that's true. But out on the moors, it wasn't just a governess you wanted. It was me.

(A beat. **AGATHA** *is – can it be? – a little uncomfortable.)*

AGATHA. Is this...conversation...a necessary part of our negotiation?

EMILIE. What assurances can you offer, regarding us?

AGATHA. There are rarely assurances to be had, in such matters.

EMILIE. No?

AGATHA. None that can be believed.

EMILIE. I disagree.

(A beat.)

AGATHA. *(Genuine.)* Are you in love, little Emilie?

EMILIE. I've never felt the way I felt when I read your letters. I've never felt that way in my whole life.

AGATHA. And when you see me face to face, and I am nothing like the man in your letters?

EMILIE. On the contrary, you are very much like him.

AGATHA. How is that?

EMILIE. The man in the letters was merciless, and you are merciless. He was overly bold, and your eyes are bold. He doled out kindness sparingly so I was hungry for it, and this is what you do as well, I know you are doing it and yet I still find myself willing to do almost anything for a moment of that kindness. The man in the letters was a strategist, Agatha, and that is exactly what you are.

*(***AGATHA** *is surprised, despite herself.)*

AGATHA. That was remarkably astute of you.

EMILIE. You thought I was stupid.

AGATHA. Educated, of course, but quite stupid.

EMILIE. And how do you feel about me now?

(A beat between them. **AGATHA** *smiles.)*

AGATHA. Come sit with me.

*(***EMILIE** *does.)*

You have made a fair number of orthographical mistakes in your letters. I have circled them for you so that you may see.

EMILIE. *(Nonplussed.)* You have...circled my mistakes?

AGATHA. If one can see one's mistakes plain in the face, one does not repeat them.

Does one.

(She looks **EMILIE** *plain in the face.)*

(Very close. Within kissing distance.)

(Giving **EMILIE** *space to decide.)*

EMILIE. This is no mistake.

*(***EMILIE** *kisses her.* **AGATHA** *gives in to the kiss. When it ends:)*

And there it is... How you're looking at me.

AGATHA. Emilie...

EMILIE. If I love you, don't mistake that for weakness.

What I'll love most is what you have to offer.

AGATHA. Very good.

EMILIE. Is it?

AGATHA. There is nothing in this world more honest and dependable than self-interest.

(Beat.)

When the clock strikes midnight, you may go upstairs to Branwell.

Until then, put your head in my lap and rest.

*(***EMILIE** *leans back against* **AGATHA**. *She produces* **HULDEY***'s diary.)*

EMILIE. This was left in the Solarium tonight.

It was left open, and I saw my name.

AGATHA. How appalling.

EMILIE. Don't you want to know what she says about us?

AGATHA. I seek to never concern myself with the inner life of my sister.

EMILIE. *(Reading.)* Monday: Emilie does nothing but stare at Agatha, do I even exist, I hate Agatha.

Tuesday: if I were to die and return in a different form, I should like to be a rat, because their lives are much much shorter.

Wednesday: Bam!

(Still reading, but surprised.)

Today is the best // day –

AGATHA. *(Takes the diary, closes it.)* Enough.

EMILIE. All right then, sing me a lullaby.

AGATHA. A lullaby!

EMILIE. I am always the one singing lullabies to children who hate me. This may be my only opportunity to have one sung to me.

AGATHA. *(With unaccustomed gentleness.)* I don't know any lullabies. I have never sung one.

EMILIE. What you do is, you think of some very simple words.

And you sing them to a very simple tune.

(Beat. **AGATHA** *thinks hard. Then she sings to* **EMILIE.** *Her voice is rusty and a little awful, but also strangely touching. She uses the melody that* **EMILIE** *sang before.)*

AGATHA.

GOOD NIGHT EMILIE
SOON YOU WILL VISIT BRANWELL IN THE ATTIC
HE IS UP IN THE ATTIC
BUT THEN YOU WILL COME BACK DOWN
AND IT WILL BE VERY NICE
YOUR BONES AND BLOOD WILL BE PART OF THIS LAND
AND THEY'LL BURY YOU HERE WHEN YOU DIE.

13.

(The **MASTIFF** *and the* **MOOR-HEN.***)*

(It's late at night.)

(He's made her a nest of straw.)

(She sits in it, sort of awkwardly.)

(The **MASTIFF** *has been talking for a long time.)*

MASTIFF. – and usually that makes me feel alienated and cut-off
but this time, I just thought it was beautiful
a little romantic, actually
and then I thought: I would do anything for you.

(Beat.)

What are you thinking?

MOOR-HEN. My leg is a lot better.

MASTIFF. Oh that's wonderful!

(Beat.)

How better?

MOOR-HEN. A lot better. I can stand. I can walk.

MASTIFF. Oh.

MOOR-HEN. What do you mean "Oh"?

MASTIFF. Nothing.

MOOR-HEN. What.

MASTIFF. It's good that you can stand and that you can walk.
But if you can stand and you can walk, maybe you can walk away from me.

(Beat.)

MOOR-HEN. But right now I'm sitting and resting.

MASTIFF. Okay.

MOOR-HEN. Right now we're both just sitting and resting.

(Beat.)

MASTIFF. I was thinking, what if I learned to fly?

MOOR-HEN. To...fly?

MASTIFF. Yes, what if I learned how to do it too, and then you could fly away if you wanted, but I could go with you, and if you crash-landed again I could help you, or also maybe if I was with you, you wouldn't crash-land.

(The **MOOR-HEN** *gives this serious thought.)*

MOOR-HEN. You? Fly?

MASTIFF. Me fly.

MOOR-HEN. I don't think you can fly.

Can you?

MASTIFF. I've never tried.

MOOR-HEN. I don't think... I mean. I'm not very educated. But I don't think I've ever seen that before.

MASTIFF. I'd do it for you. If you wanted me to.

MOOR-HEN. Let me think about that.

MASTIFF. Do you not want me to go with you? Do you not want me with you all the time?

MOOR-HEN. Well maybe not *all* the time.

I mean.

There's privacy.

MASTIFF. I hate privacy. Everything is always already private anyway. I want to be so close to you that it feels like my skin is going to explode.

(Beat.)

MOOR-HEN. Maybe you could fly a little bit behind me, sometimes.

So you could still see me, but I'd have privacy.

MASTIFF. I guess I could do that.

(Beat – sad.)

I don't think I can fly.

(Beat – tentative.)

Maybe you could not fly.

MOOR-HEN. What?

MASTIFF. Maybe you could not fly.

MOOR-HEN. Not...fly.

MASTIFF. Maybe – I don't know, I'm just bouncing ideas around here –

Maybe you could just kind of. Walk. From now on.

And I could walk next to you.

MOOR-HEN. Walk?

I'm bad at walking.

I limp.

MASTIFF. Or I could walk a step or two behind you, but if you stumbled at all, I'd catch you immediately.

MOOR-HEN. Wait a minute...

MASTIFF. Or actually, if you sat in a little wagon? With wheels? I could push you.

So you wouldn't have to walk.

MOOR-HEN. But what if I wanted to?

MASTIFF. If you wanted to walk, you could walk.

MOOR-HEN. But what if I wanted to fly?

(Beat.)

*(***MASTIFF*** is depressed but also upset.)*

(Even if he tries to keep a lid on it.)

MASTIFF. I just don't understand why you'd want to do something I couldn't do when there are lots of other things you could do that I *can* do. Unless you haven't been happy with me. Have you not been happy?

MOOR-HEN. That's not what I'm saying.

MASTIFF. *(Losing it a little.)* Then I don't understand what you're saying. Because you hate flying! So if you are wanting to do something that I can't do, that you hate, it must be because you want to get away from me!

MOOR-HEN. I just. I am something. That flies. That's all.

MASTIFF. Sorry.

I'm sorry.

I don't mean to be crazy.

You just

you mean so much

you have no idea.

MOOR-HEN. I'm not saying you're crazy. But it freaks me out when you get intense.

MASTIFF. Sorry, I'm sorry.

MOOR-HEN. Don't be sorry, just be calm.

MASTIFF. Okay.

Calm. Okay.

(Beat – an outburst again.)

I just, I have this nightmare where I turn my back for a second and then I feel this *tug*, inside me somewhere inside my heart somewhere, and I turn around but it's too late, you're *rising* into the sky, you're just drifting away from me and I can't reach you and you won't come back down and all I can do is watch you get smaller and smaller and smaller until the moors have swallowed you completely and you're gone.

(Beat.)

MOOR-HEN. I'm right here.

MASTIFF. *Now*. You're right here *now*.

MOOR-HEN. I am right here. Now.

MASTIFF. What about tomorrow?

MOOR-HEN. You're getting intense again.

MASTIFF. Sorry.

Sorry.

(Beat.)

I don't ever want to feel the way I felt before I met you.

MOOR-HEN. But sometimes you will. Sometimes you will feel like that.

MASTIFF. Not if you don't fly away from me!

MOOR-HEN. Even if I don't fly away from you, there will be a moment in which you look at my face, and it isn't the face you thought you were looking at, maybe it has an expression that you don't recognize. Or you'll hear something about my past that you didn't know, that will make you wonder if you really know me. And then, for that time, for however long it lasts, you will feel like a squashed grub again.

(Beat. **MASTIFF** *really looks at her.)*

MASTIFF. Then you should tell me everything about yourself now. And I'll learn all your expressions. And then I'll never feel that way.

MOOR-HEN. I don't think you're really hearing what I'm saying.

MASTIFF. Come here. Sit very close to me and tell me everything.

MOOR-HEN. Actually. I'd like to be here. And you can be there. And maybe we can be quiet for a little bit.

MASTIFF. I can feel you drifting away. I can feel a distance between us.

Why is there a distance between us?

MOOR-HEN. Because sometimes there is a distance. Because this is a place built on distance. And that's okay.

MASTIFF. It's horrible. I feel horrible. Hold onto me.

MOOR-HEN. Breathe.

Okay?

Take deep breaths.

Count.

Breathe in the shape of a square.

Calm down.

(The **MASTIFF** *calms down.)*

(When he's calm he looks at her.)

(New determination. Almost scary.)

MASTIFF. I won't let it happen.

MOOR-HEN. What?

MASTIFF. I won't let you drift away from me.

14.

(The Great Hall...which looks the same as the parlor. Late that same night. **AGATHA** *is alone, waiting for* **EMILIE** *to return from the attic. Perhaps she paces. Perhaps she sits.)*

*(***HULDEY** *enters. She's dressed unusually well. She carries a small axe behind her back. She keeps it out of sight of* **AGATHA** *at all times.)*

HULDEY. There you are!

AGATHA. You.

HULDEY. I've been looking for you. And here you are, in the Great Hall.

AGATHA. I should think you would be asleep.

HULDEY. I should think *you* would be asleep.

(Beat.)

Where have you been all evening?

AGATHA. I was feeling...unwell.

HULDEY. And where has Emilie been?

AGATHA. I imagine Miss Vandergaard was also feeling... unwell.

(Beat.)

Were you playing dress-up?

HULDEY. Why can't you just say that I look nice?

AGATHA. If I meant to say that you looked nice, I would have said that you looked nice.

(Beat.)

HULDEY. One of my diaries has gone missing tonight.

AGATHA. Oh?

HULDEY. I looked for it everywhere, I couldn't find it.

AGATHA. You must have misplaced it.

*(***HULDEY** *watches her, clutching her axe.)*

HULDEY. Sister.

AGATHA. Yes, sister.

HULDEY. I am very. very. unhappy.

AGATHA. Is that so.

HULDEY. Yes it is, it is so now, and it has always been so.

AGATHA. That doesn't make you special.

HULDEY. ...What?

AGATHA. Everybody is very very unhappy, Huldey. It is simply what things are. The land is bleak and the house is large and there is no language for all the things lurking within us, no matter how much we write in our diaries, and we are all quite unhappy. So what.

(Beat. **HULDEY** *didn't expect this.)*

(She might lower or put down the axe, which **AGATHA** *still has not seen.)*

HULDEY. Are *you*...unhappy?

AGATHA. I have achieved balance.

HULDEY. Balance?

AGATHA. I do not strive for happiness. Which has made me less unhappy.

I set goals for myself, and I achieve those goals.

You might try it, if you weren't scribbling in your diary all the time.

HULDEY. But what if... I mean. Aren't there. Other ways?

AGATHA. And what would those "other ways" be?

HULDEY. If something amazing happened. Something wild or spectacular or completely unexpected. Don't you think it would make us happy?

(The briefest of beats. And then:)

AGATHA. No.

HULDEY. Why not?

AGATHA. Because then that event would be over. The wild, spectacular – whatever it was. And then you would be alone again, only this time you would not have achieved balance, you would have achieved expectation. You would want to feel that way again and again, more and more, and you would *not* feel that way again and again more and more, and so you would be. even. more. unhappy.

(Now the axe has definitely been put down.)

HULDEY. *(But not meanly – almost searchingly.)* I think I hate you.

AGATHA. I know that.

HULDEY. You do?

AGATHA. I read your diary.

HULDEY. *(A little delighted.)* You did?

AGATHA. I did.

HULDEY. And what did you think of it?

AGATHA. I thought it was of very poor quality.

(**HULDEY** *is crushed.)*

HULDEY. You...did?

AGATHA. I am sorry to say that I did.

HULDEY. And...why? Why did you feel that way?

AGATHA. There was monotony, repetition, poor attention to detail, a plaintive narrator's voice that did little to endear itself with the reader, your spelling could improve immensely – to be honest I'm shocked that it hasn't – but mostly, to be candid, it was boring.

HULDEY. *(White-faced.)* Boring?

AGATHA. Quite quite
boring.

(A beat.)

(And then **HULDEY** *launches herself at* **AGATHA.***)*

(This was entirely unplanned.)

(She is fueled by sheer rage and hurt.)

(She hits **AGATHA** *in the head with a heavy object. Perhaps a vase? Not the axe.)*

*(***AGATHA** *falls.)*

*(***HULDEY** *keeps hitting her, blind with rage.)*

HULDEY. I
AM
NOT
BORING!!!
I
AM
FAMOUS!
I
AM
SO
FAMOUS!
I
HAVE
A
SONG!!
ABOUT
ME!
NOBODY
ELSE
HERE
HAS
A
SONG!

(Beat. She looks at **AGATHA. AGATHA** *is quite dead.* **HULDEY** *has no idea what to do.)*

...Agatha?
Agatha.
Agatha?

(A beat. There's blood all over her. [She's shaking.])

Oh.

Well.
Oh.

(She has no idea what to do.)

Marjory?
Mallory!
Marjory!!
Mallory!!

(Nobody comes. She has no idea.)

Oh!
Well.
I am going to sing my song now.

(Beat.)

(This starts off melodiously sung.)

(Then turns into a crazy rock power-ballad.)

(Fog and lights and blood and madness.)

[Cue: "Huldey's Power Ballad"]

THERE'S A HAUNTING WIND ON THE MOORS TONIGHT
THERE'S A BLOOD-RED MOON SO BOLD
THEY'LL ALL BUILD FIRES IN THEIR HEARTHS TONIGHT
BUT MINE ALONE STANDS COLD.

THERE'S A DRIVING RAIN ON THE MOORS TONIGHT
FRAGILE HAWKS AND LITTLE HARES MUST HIDE
THERE'S A BITING COLD IN THE AIR TONIGHT
BUT I ALONE DON'T MIND.

MURDER IS A COLOR LIKE THE HEAT OF THE DAY
MURDER IS THE GENTLEMAN YOU WISH WOULD STAY
MURDER IS THE ORANGE DRESS YOU THOUGHT YOU
COULDN'T AFFORD
A MURDERESS, YOU KNOW, IS NEVER BORED.

MURDER IS A COLOR LIKE THE DEEPEST SUMMER SKY
MURDER IS A BABY BIRD WHO SUDDENLY LEARNED TO FLY
MURDER IS A WOMAN'S MOST PRESTIGIOUS AWARD
AND A MURDERESS, I SAY, IS NEVER BORED.

I DID A THING, A VERY BAD THING
I CHOPPED HER HEAD WITH ONE GREAT SWING
I BEAT HER DEAD TILL SHE WAS GORY
...I'M NOT SORRY

I DID A THING, A VERY BAD THING
I CHOPPED HER HEAD WITH ONE GREAT SWING
I BEAT HER DEAD TILL SHE WAS GORY
...I'M NOT SORRY

(Rap section.)

THE AXE WENT WHACK AND THEN HER SKULL WENT CRICK-A-CRACK-CRACK
HERE'S A DRIPPY-DRIP AS HER BLOOD GOES SPLIT-A-SPLAT-SPLAT
AND CREE-CREE-CREE GOES THE OWL IN THE DARK OF NIGHT
WHOO-WHOO WHO WILL COME FOR YOU, IT'S YOU-KNOW-WHO: A MURDERESS IS NIGH!

(Singing again.)

I DID A THING, A VERY BAD THING
I CHOPPED HER HEAD WITH ONE GREAT SWING
I BEAT HER DEAD TILL SHE WAS GORY
...I'M NOT SORRY!!

*(**HULDEY** reaches the end of it.)*

(A sea of applause crashes over her.)

(It is the sweetest sound she has ever heard.)

*(It nourishes her like sunlight to a starving plant. She bathes in it. Slowly, the applause filters away. Slowly, we start to hear rain instead, and wild wind. There is no applause. There is a storm outside. **HULDEY** doesn't feel this shift at first.)*

Thank you
thank you
yes I am
yes I did
yes and I feel nothing.

Oh it means so much to see you all here tonight
thank you, thank you...

(Feeling the shift.)

Wait.
Wait.
Where did you go?
Come back!

(She opens the door and rain drives in.)

(She dashes out onto the moors and is devoured by them.)

15.

(The Great Hall…which continues to look very much like the parlor. Next morning.)

(A gigantic bloodstain on the floor. **MARJORY***'s diary sits on* **AGATHA***'s chair.)*

*(***EMILIE** *stands in front of the bloodstain. She has just entered. She stares at it, in horror. The sound of someone coming.* **EMILIE** *sits down in the chair, diary in hand, and composes her face.* **MARJORY** *enters with a mop and bucket.)*

MARJORY. Oh.

EMILIE. Mallory.

MARJORY. I didn't know anyone was in here.

EMILIE. I'm in here.

MARJORY. I can see that.

(Beat – staring at the stain.)

I was just going to…dust.

EMILIE. Were you?

MARJORY. The Great Hall has fallen into…disarray.

EMILIE. Oh, I hadn't noticed.

(A beat between them. **MARJORY** *puts the mop and bucket aside.)*

MARJORY. I can see you found my diary.

EMILIE. Is this your diary?

MARJORY. It is.

EMILIE. I thought it was Huldey's diary.

MARJORY. It was Huldey's diary and then it became my diary.

EMILIE. Oh.

(A beat.)

MARJORY. Have you seen Miss Huldey this morning?

EMILIE. I?

MARJORY. Yes.

EMILIE. No.

No doubt she's taking a long walk on the moors.

MARJORY. No doubt.

EMILIE. Are you looking for her?

MARJORY. No, not I.

EMILIE. Have you seen Miss Agatha?

MARJORY. No, I can't say that I have.

Why, are you looking for her?

EMILIE. I? No no.

MARJORY. Are you sure?

EMILIE. I'm quite content, thank you.

I have no need of either.

(A beat between them.)

MARJORY. You look different.

EMILIE. I do?

MARJORY. Somehow you do.

EMILIE. Well. Isn't that something.

(Beat.)

MARJORY. You might read out loud.

EMILIE. But it's your diary, Mallory, you know what it says.

MARJORY. Margaret.

EMILIE. Excuse me?

MARJORY. I'm "Margaret." When I'm an author.

EMILIE. Oh.

(Reads out loud.)

"Monday: Everything shall always be different now. And yet nothing changes in this bleak land. I once saw a kitten ripped apart by savage birds. It seemed that such an awful thing would change the face of the land forever. And yet, when it was over, there was no sign that it had occurred, save a little bit of fur caught in the gorse."

(To **MARJORY.***)*

EMILIE. Quite good, Margaret, really.

MARJORY. That's very kind.

EMILIE. Did that actually happen?

MARJORY. Oh. I'm not sure. It's hard to tell.

EMILIE. I understand perfectly.
You might say a "scrap" of fur.

MARJORY. "Scrap"?

EMILIE. It's a better word than "bit."

MARJORY. "Save a little scrap of fur."
Oh. That is better.

EMILIE. The alliteration, you see.

MARJORY. Yes, that's nice.

(The door opens. Both women look.)

(The **MASTIFF** *walks in.)*

(He is covered in blood.)

(Feathers stuck to the blood.)

(He walks straight past them and goes to sit by the fire. He stares blankly into the fire.)

EMILIE. What on earth has happened to the dog.

MARJORY. It must have gone hunting, I imagine.

EMILIE. It must have caught something.

MARJORY. I suppose it must.

EMILIE. Sit down, Margaret. Here's a pen.
Read it all again, and let us make some judicious alterations.

*(***MARJORY** *takes the pen. She takes the diary.)*

(She sits. **EMILIE** *watches her keenly.)*

MARJORY. Monday: Everything shall always be different now. And yet nothing changes...

EMILIE. Oh yes.

That's good.
That's very good.

(Lights down.)

End of Play

The Moors

Music by Daniel Kluger
Lyrics by Jen Silverman

Emilie's Song

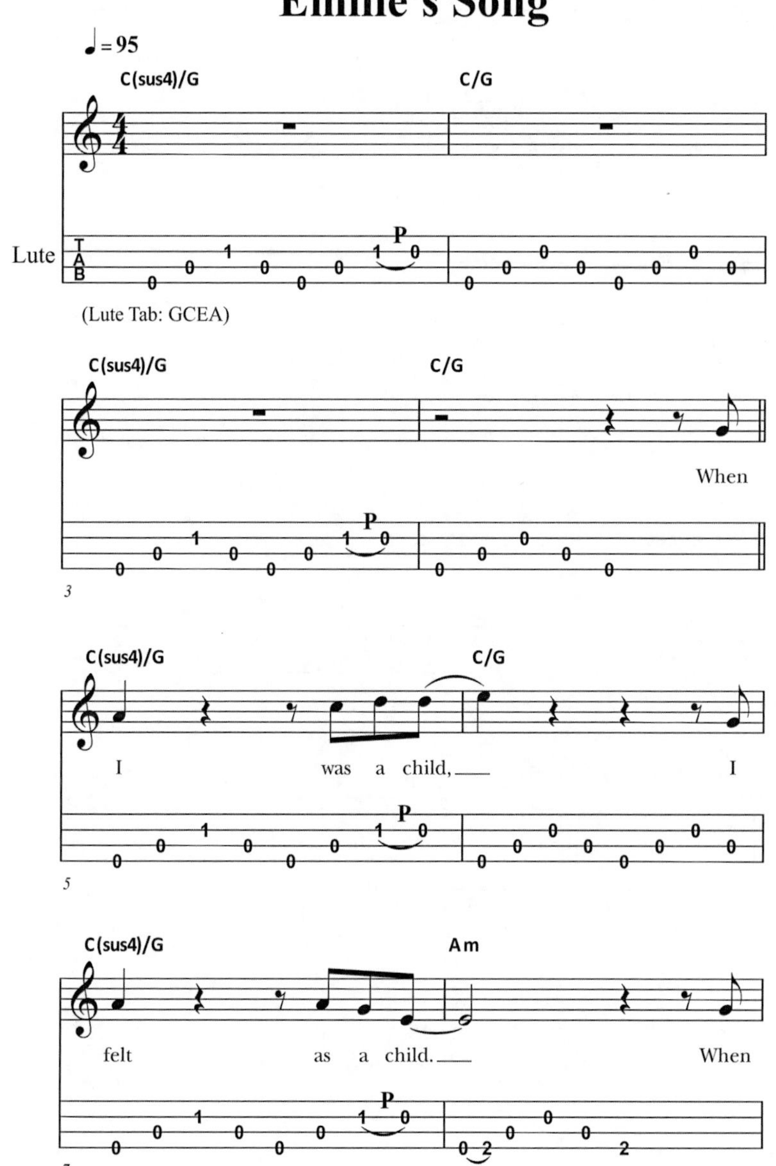

C(sus4)/G
C/G
I was a wo - man, I
9
C(sus4)/G
Am
felt some-thing new. When
11
C7/B♭
Am
I be-come old, I'll
13
C+/G♯
D
turn to bone or hea - ther. When I
15
G6
F
die the winds will cry but the
17

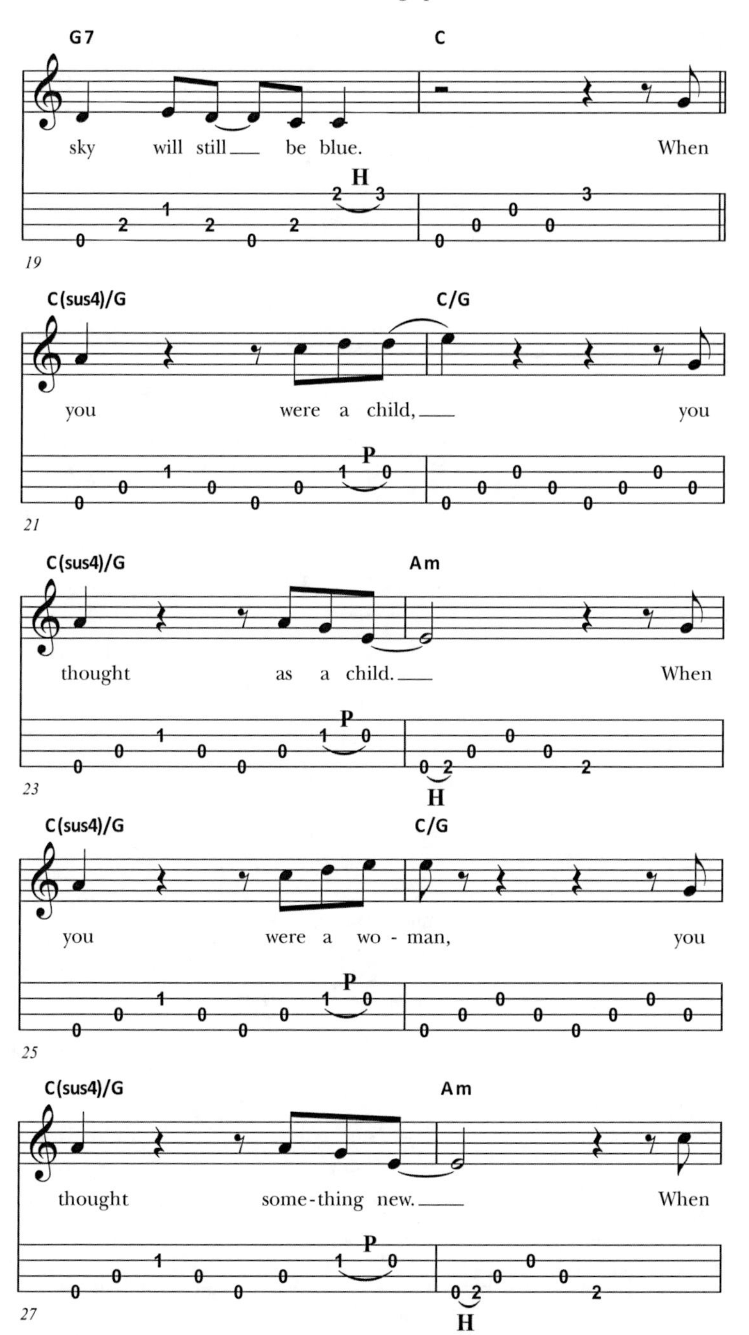
G7
C
sky will still be blue.
When
H
19
C(sus4)/G
C/G
you were a child,
you
P
21
C(sus4)/G
Am
thought as a child.
When
P
H
23
C(sus4)/G
C/G
you were a wo - man,
you
P
25
C(sus4)/G
Am
thought some-thing new.
When
P
H
27

C7/B♭
Am
you be - come old, you'll
29
C+/G♯
D
change just like the wea - ther. When you
31
G6
F
die the winds will cry, but the
P
33
G7
C
sun will still shine through.
H
35
C(sus4)/G
Am
There's a haunt-ing wind on the moors to - night.
P
H
37

C(sus4)/G
Am
There's a blood red moon so bold.
P
H
39
C(sus4)/G
Am
They will all build fires in the hearths to-night,
P
H
41
C(sus4)/G
Am
butmine a-lone stands cold.
P
H
43
C(sus4)/G
Am
There's a bit-ing cold in the air to-night,
P
H
45
C(sus4)/G
Am
but I a-lone don't mind.
P
H
47

C(sus4)/G
C/G
Oh, for a life where we're
P
49
C(sus4)/G
Am
sim - ple as the stars.
P
H
51
C(sus4)/G
C/G
Oh, for a life where we're
P
53
C(sus4)/G
Am
free - er than the grass.
P
H
55
C7/B♭
Am
Oh, for a life where we're
57

C+/G♯
D
bold - er than the day - break. And
59
G6
F
oh, for a life.
where,
P
61
G7
C
like the time, we pass.
H
63

The Moors

Music by Daniel Kluger
Lyrics by Jen Silverman

Huldey's Power Ballad

17
Cm
Eb
There's a bit - ing cold in the air to-night
19
Ab
Db
but I al - one don't mind. Mur-
21
Dm/F
der is a col - or like the heat of day, Mur -
22
Gm
der is the gent-le-man you wish would stay, Mur -
23
F/A
der is the o - range dress you thought you
24
G7sus/C
G7/D
could-n't af - ford A
25
A7
G/B
A7/C♯ B7
mur-der-ess, you know, is ne-ver bored. Mur-
27
Em/G
der is a col-or like the deep-est summ-er sky, Mur -

28
Am
der is a bab-y bird who sudd-en-ly learned to fly, Mur-
29
G/B
A/C♯
der is a wom-an's most pres-ti-gious a-ward
A
31
B7
A/C♯
B7/D♯ F/E♭
mur-der-ess (I say!) is nev-er bored.
33
B♭m
G♭/B♭
ff
I did a thing, a ver-y bad thing
35
B♭m
G♭/B♭
I chopped her head with one great swing
37
B♭m
G♭/B♭
I beat her dead till she was gor-y
39
G
E
I'm not sor-ry.
41
B♭m
G♭/B♭
I did a thing, a ver-y bad thing

43
B♭m
G♭/B♭
I chopped her head with one great swing

45
B♭m
G♭/B♭
I cut her up and earned my glor - y

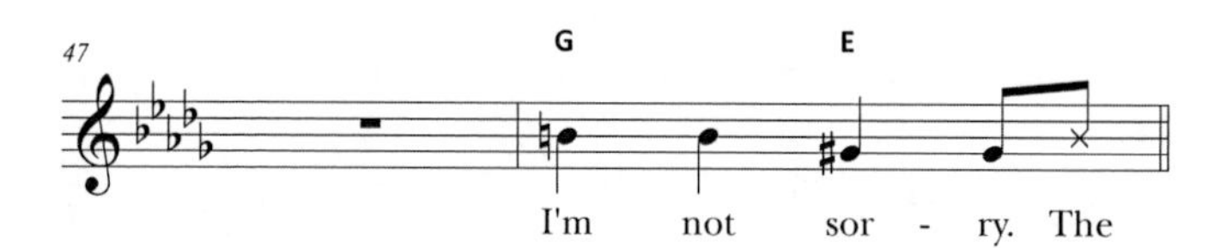
47
G
E
I'm not sor - ry. The

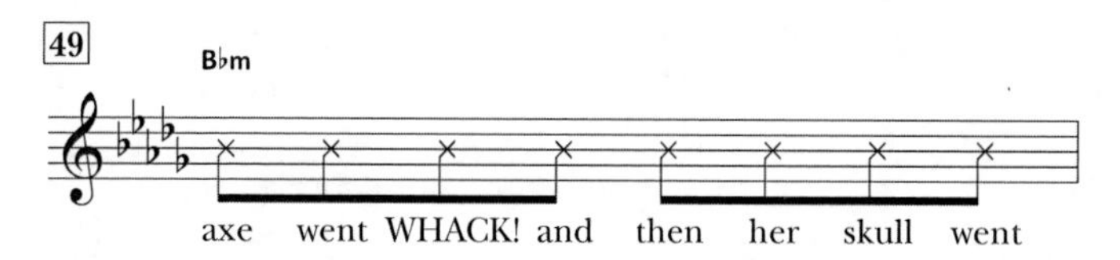
49
B♭m
axe went WHACK! and then her skull went

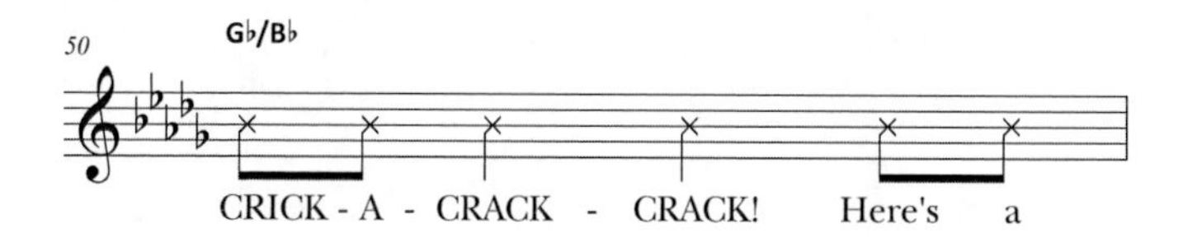
50
G♭/B♭
CRICK - A - CRACK - CRACK! Here's a

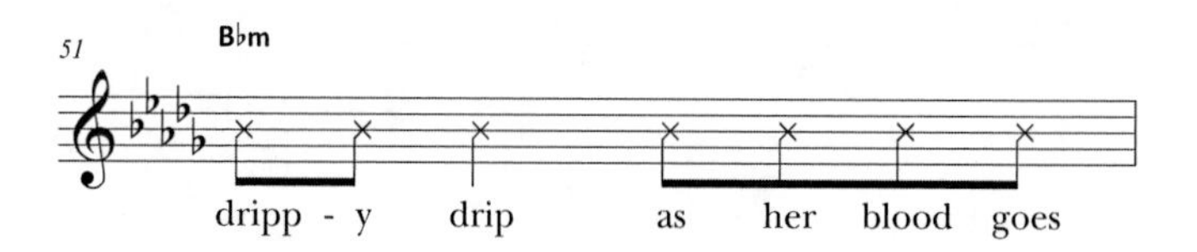
51
B♭m
dripp - y drip as her blood goes

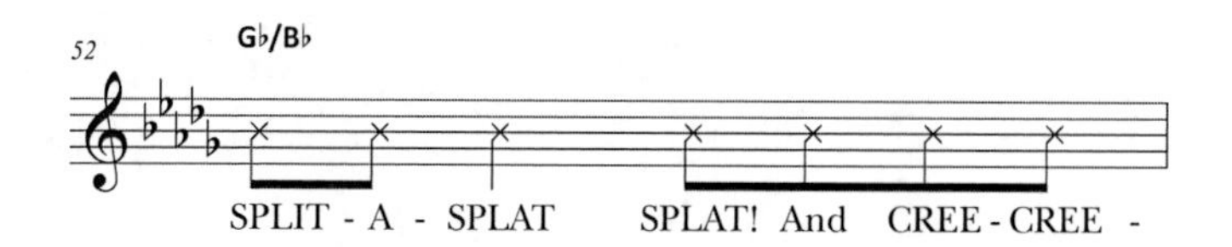
52
G♭/B♭
SPLIT - A - SPLAT SPLAT! And CREE - CREE -

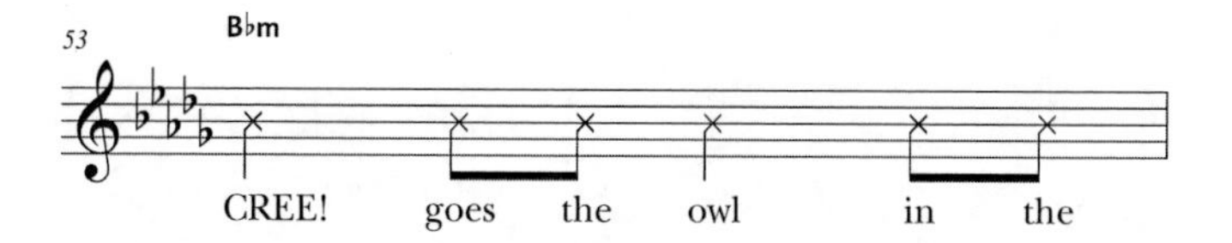
53
B♭m
CREE! goes the owl in the

54
G♭/B♭
dark of night. WHOO - WHOO -

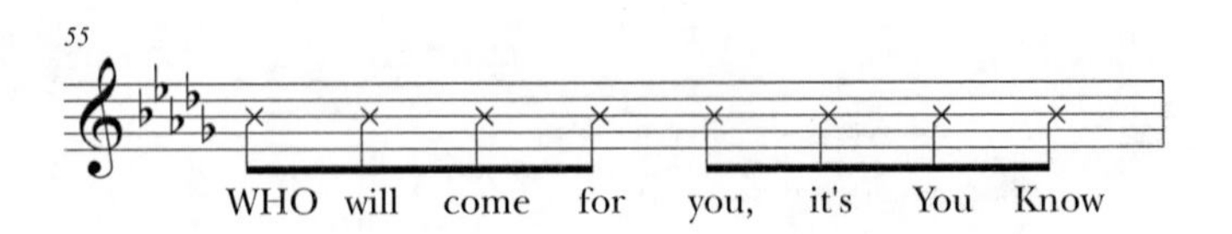
55
WHO will come for you, it's You Know

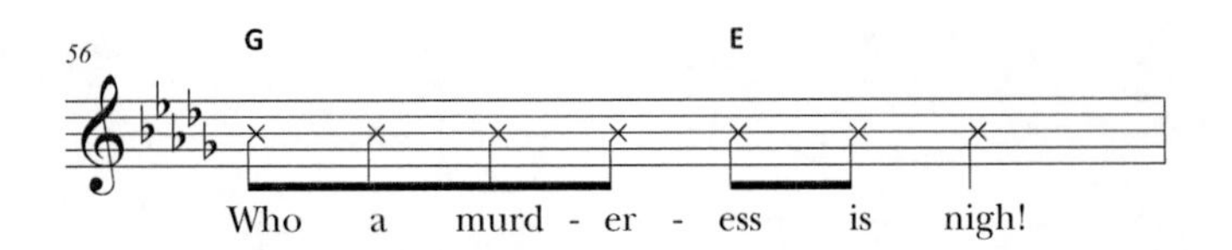
56
G
E
Who a murd - er - ess is nigh!

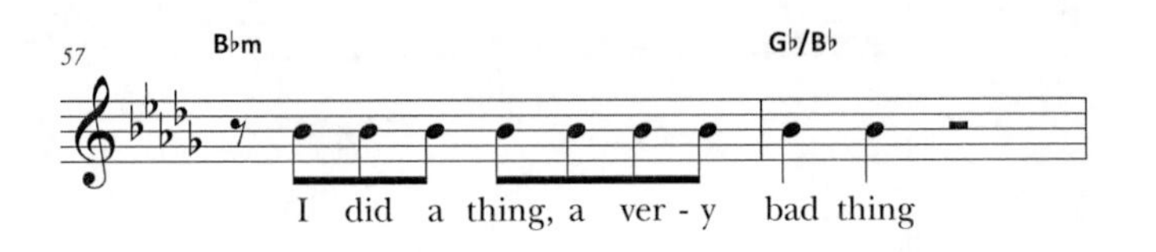
57
B♭m
G♭/B♭
I did a thing, a ver - y bad thing

59
B♭m
G♭/B♭
I chopped her head with one great swing

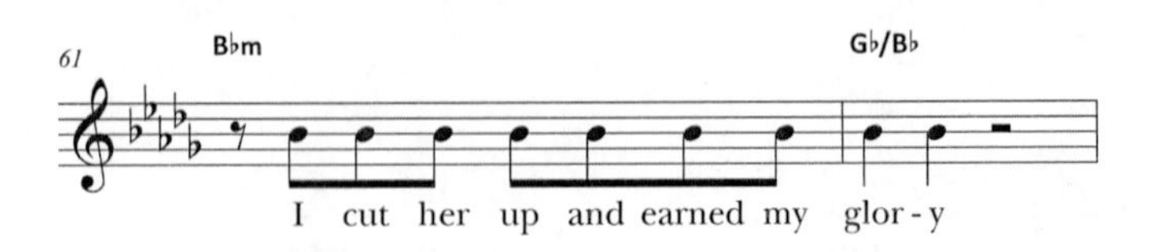
61
B♭m
G♭/B♭
I cut her up and earned my glor - y

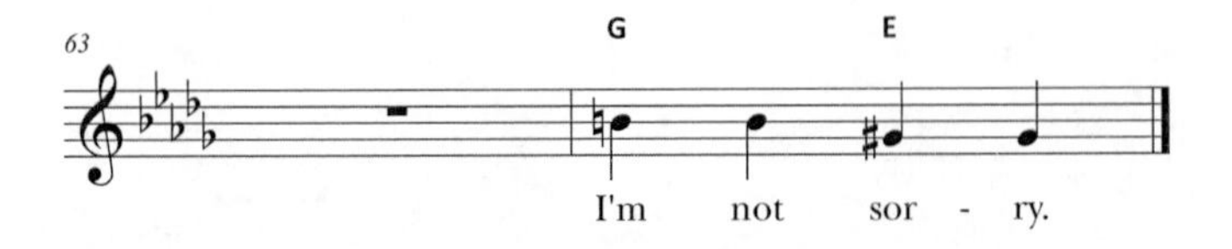
63
G
E
I'm not sor - ry.